I ♥ Band!

Friends, Fugues, and Fortune Cookies

by Michelle Schusterman

Grosset & Dunlap
An Imprint of Penguin Group (USA) LLC

GROSSET & DUNLAP
Published by the Penguin Group
Penguin Group (USA) LLC, 375 Hudson Street, New York, New York 10014, USA

USA | Canada | UK | Ireland | Australia | New Zealand | India | South Africa | China

penguin.com
A Penguin Random House Company

Cover illustration by Genevieve Kote.

Library of Congress Cataloging-in-Publication Data is available.

ISBN 978-0-448-45684-3   10 9 8 7 6 5 4 3 2 1

For old (but strong)
Flower Mound friendships

Chapter One

*W*inning isn't everything.

I tell myself that a lot. Sometimes I believe it, too.

Like with friendships—that's a red light. Getting too competitive with a friend is a good way to make an enemy.

Then there's stuff like band—yellow light. Proceed with caution. Winning is great, but it's not the only thing that matters.

And then there's video games, like *Prophet Wars*—major green light. It's total galaxy-wide domination or go home.

The problem is, *everything's* a green light for me, at least at first. It's like an instinct. That's why, when my band director decided to make our fund-raiser a competition, my first thought was that my bandmates were going down like an alien airship flying over my level-three jungle subterranean missile silo.

What? Maybe winning isn't everything, but it's still pretty awesome.

It was fourth period at Millican Middle School, which meant I was in the band hall for advanced band rehearsal. Last week, Mr. Dante had announced that we would be going to New Orleans for a band contest in March. And *that* meant four days of staying up late in hotel rooms, competing at a big band contest at an amusement park, and missing classes. To help pay for the trip, the band was going to hold a bake sale.

Mr. Dante pushed his glasses up his nose and looked around the band hall. "As some of you might know, our girls' volleyball team is in the playoffs," he said. "Three of their tournaments are going to be held in our gym, and Coach Reyes has agreed to allow us to sell concessions during the games. We're going to split into teams—woodwind, brass, and percussion." He held up a finger when Derrick Adler raised his hand from where he stood behind a xylophone.

"Don't worry," Mr. Dante said. "I'm aware that this isn't an even match as far as how many students are on each team. That's why I'm not judging this by the total amount of money you make. Instead, the winning section will be the one that averages the most money raised per student. The important thing here is that you work together as a team."

On my right, Natasha Prynne raised her hand.

"What does the winning section get?" she asked, and I couldn't help but grin. Natasha was pretty much as competitive as me, which was why she sat next to me as first chair in our section. She was also one of my best friends. (See? I could handle not winning. Sometimes.)

"Glad you asked," Mr. Dante said, smiling. "The section that wins will actually get two prizes. First, they'll get to decide on the final design for the new T-shirts I'm going to order for our trip to New Orleans."

Trevor Wells's hand shot up. "You mean like we can pick any design at all?" he asked. I rolled my eyes. Knowing Trevor, he was probably picturing us in band T-shirts covered in wizards or dragons or something equally lame.

"Within reason," Mr. Dante told him. "As for the other prize . . ." He cleared his throat. "At my last school, I had a tradition of dressing as Santa to conduct the advanced band at the winter concert."

"Santa?" Gabby Flores said in disbelief, then caught herself and raised her hand. Mr. Dante nodded at her. "Santa?" she repeated, and several kids giggled. "Are you serious? Why?"

"Because I'm a jolly person," Mr. Dante said with a perfectly straight face. Now I was laughing, too.

Mr. Dante looked a little miffed. "Anyway, I thought maybe I could start a new tradition here at Millican. I'll still dress as Santa at the winter concert, but the winning section can choose to alter or add to my costume however they'd like." He paused. "Again, within reason."

A voice behind me caused my stomach to flutter. "You mean, we could make you zombie Santa?" asked Aaron Cook, and several students laughed.

"That's the idea," Mr. Dante replied. "But remember—"

"Vampire Santa!" exclaimed Sophie Wheeler.

Gabby grinned. "Hippie Santa!"

My best friend, Julia Gordon, caught my eye from the clarinet section. "How about Mrs. Claus?" she called with a wicked grin, and everyone cracked up.

Mr. Dante held his hands up, but he was smiling, too. "Whatever the costume, it has to be approved by the band boosters. And speaking of," he added, holding up a stack of papers, "I need you all to take these home to your parents. We'll need a few of them to volunteer, both at the volleyball games and with any baking your section does."

Natasha leaned closer to me as he passed out the papers. "Not good. I tried baking cookies once— we ended up feeding them to the neighbor's dog," she whispered, and I grinned.

"Hang on, I've got an idea." After making sure Mr. Dante was still handing out papers, I leaned back and reached behind Brooke Dennis, tapping Owen Reynolds on the shoulder.

Owen was fourth-chair horn. His real talent was drawing. Well, that and *Prophets*. We hung out at his house every Thursday afternoon to blow up virtual aliens. Last week, his mom had made us these amazing cream-cheese brownies to celebrate that we finally got to level four.

"Do you think your mom could help us?" I asked softly. "Those brownies, maybe?"

Owen nodded. "I'll ask her."

Smiling, I turned back to Natasha. "Owen's mom will help us. I know she'll say yes."

"Cool," said Natasha. "Hey, how are you doing on the all-region music?"

Wrinkling my nose, I pulled Fugue in F Minor out of my folder and set it on my music stand. "Not bad. I'm still having trouble near the end, right here," I said, pointing.

Natasha nodded. "Yeah, that part's really hard. Want to work on it together sometime?"

Mr. Dante was getting back up on the podium, so I just nodded in response. All-region auditions were in a few weeks. Band students from all seven middle schools in the Oak Point School District could audition to be in one of the two all-region bands. In February, they'd get to miss an entire day of school to go to rehearsal with a guest conductor, and then they'd perform at a concert.

Two bands meant a total of eight French horn spots, and who knew how many horn players in the district would be auditioning. It would be tough to make it, but Natasha and I were going to try. Especially since Mr. Dante had decided that the all-region results would count as our next chair test.

Natasha grabbed her pencil and scrawled

something on the bottom of my étude.

Tomorrow after school?

I gave her a thumbs-up.

While Mr. Dante tuned the flutes one at a time, I studied the étude, tapping my fingers. Natasha was an amazing horn player and a good friend, but all-region was a yellow light, and I was going to do my best to make it.

"I swear, Holly, I'm still having nightmares."

I pressed my lips together to keep from laughing. Julia glared at me.

"I'm serious!" she cried. "You said it wouldn't be that scary."

"No, I said it wouldn't be that *gory*," I replied, grinning. Last weekend for Halloween, my brother Chad and I went to the Asylum—ranked the third-best haunted house in Austin. And since he was meeting a bunch of his friends there, I'd convinced him to let me bring Julia and Natasha, too.

Or maybe *drag* would be a better word.

"The worst part was the clowns," Julia said, shuddering as we skirted around a group of eighth-grade girls and headed into C-hall.

"Really?" I asked. "I thought the scariest part was when we were crammed in that tiny room and the guy crawled across the ceiling."

Julia stopped, her eyes round. "What?"

"You don't remember?"

She started walking again, brow furrowed. "I remember the tiny room, and I remember the scratching noises. But I had my eyes closed."

I smiled. "That's probably a good thing."

"Someone *crawled across the ceiling*? Over our *heads*?" I didn't respond, and Julia groaned. "Never again, Holly. Seriously."

A flyer on the wall right outside the computer lab caught my eye. "Hey, look!" I grabbed Julia's arm and pointed.

"Oh yeah, the winter dance!" she exclaimed. "I totally forgot to tell you, I saw them putting up flyers in the gym today, too."

"Really?" I gave her an innocent look as we headed to our computers. "During PE?"

Julia rolled her eyes, blushing. "Yes, during PE. And no, I didn't talk to Seth."

I pressed the power button on my computer, then swiveled my chair around to face Julia. "You should ask him to the dance."

She snorted. "Yeah, right."

"I'm serious!" I insisted. "He likes you, Julia. But he's so shy, he'll never ask."

I didn't know Seth Anderson really well. We had math together in sixth grade, but he hardly ever talked. All I knew about him was that he played cello in the orchestra and he couldn't say hi to my best friend without stammering.

Julia shook her head as she typed in her password. "Probably. But that doesn't make it any easier for me to ask him."

"What's so hard?" I said. "'Hey, Seth, would you go to the winter dance with me?' Done."

Julia gave me a withering look. "Okay, if it's so easy, why don't you do it?"

I blinked. "Ask Seth to the dance for you? That's—"

"No!" Julia interrupted, laughing. "I mean ask Aaron, you dork."

Now it was my turn to blush. I'd had a crush on Aaron since the first day of seventh grade. Okay, fine, since last year. But it was still a huge accomplishment when I managed to talk to him without turning tomato red. That was his fault, though. Him and his dark brown eyes. And his smile with the creases like parentheses in his cheeks. And his—

"Hello?" Julia waved her hand in front of my face, giggling when I jumped. "So, yes or no?"

"Yes or no what?"

"You know what. Will you ask him?" She arched an eyebrow. "Since it's so easy and all."

Ugh. She was right—the thought of asking Aaron to the winter dance made me kind of nauseated.

But a tiny part of me was excited at the thought, too. I tapped my fingers on the arm of my chair.

"The dance isn't till December," I said, thinking out loud. "It's too early to ask anyone."

"True."

"So how's this," I went on. "We make a pact."

"Why do I get the feeling I'm not going to like this?" Julia closed her eyes like she was bracing herself.

"We wait till Thanksgiving break," I said. "If Seth hasn't asked you, you'll ask him. Same with me and Aaron. Deal?"

Julia squinted at me with one eye. "You're serious, aren't you?"

"Come on!" I said encouragingly. "Thanksgiving's not for a month. Plenty of time to prepare."

"You'll really do it, though?" Julia asked. "If I ask Seth to the dance, you'll ask Aaron?"

I smiled, ignoring the butterflies flapping around my stomach. "Yeah, I'll do it."

"Okay." Julia grinned at me. "It's a deal."

Chapter Two

*A*sking Aaron Cook to the winter dance. No big deal. I could totally handle it.

That's what I kept telling myself, anyway.

I waved to Mr. Dante as I headed to the practice rooms before school Thursday morning. I knew Fugue in F Minor by heart, but I still couldn't get through it without flubbing at least a few notes. There were four measures near the end that tripped me up every time. Natasha and I had worked on it together after school on Tuesday. She was struggling with it, too, and as much as I hated to admit it, I was kind of relieved. It's not always easy being friends with first chair in your section when you want to be first chair, too.

At eight thirty, I put my horn back in its case, annoyed. I'd sounded better Tuesday. I was getting *worse*. Scowling, I shoved the case into my cubby, turned around, and ran smack into someone. Someone who smelled really, really good. Kind of like grapefruit and pine trees.

"Sorry, Holly!"

Aaron grabbed my arm to steady me. His face was just a few inches away. I opened and closed my mouth a few times, but it was like my brain forgot how to send words to my mouth.

He let go, then starting pulling stuff out of his cubby (which I couldn't help but notice was a complete mess). "I think I left my history book in here," he explained, his voice muffled.

"Oh."

Yeah, asking Aaron to the dance would be no big deal for the girl standing here like a love-struck statue. Staring at his profile, I imagined saying it: *Aaron, would you go to the winter dance with me?*

And in about two seconds, I heard, like, a thousand responses.

I'm already going with someone.

I don't have a date yet, but . . . no way.

Are you serious? (That one included hysterical laughter.)

They only got worse from there.

"Did you go?"

I realized with a start that Aaron was talking to me. "What?"

He pointed at my band folder, which was covered in Asylum stickers I'd bought on Saturday. "That's the haunted house in Austin, right?"

"Oh yeah!" I said. "It was awesome."

"Really?" Aaron grinned, and I struggled not to

giggle or blush. "It didn't freak you out?"

I shrugged. "Nah, I like that kind of stuff. Julia and Natasha hated it, though."

He laughed. "Man, I wish I could've gone. My parents would never let me, though."

"Why not?" I asked, watching him resume digging through his cubby.

"They're just strict about that kind of thing." Aaron's voice was muffled. "Same with movies. I tried to go see *House of the Wicked* last month, and my mom freaked out." He straightened, shoving his history book into his backpack.

"You *have* to see it!" I exclaimed, all nerves forgotten. "It's amazing. Maybe my favorite movie of all time. Or at least, my favorite new one. I love the classics, like *Psycho*."

"I saw a little over half of *The Exorcist* on TV when I was nine," Aaron said with a grin. "My mom walked in right when the girl starts spewing green stuff everywhere. She grounded me for a week."

I laughed. "Did you ever get to finish it?"

"Nope. Hey, have you seen *Scattered*?" Aaron asked as we left the band hall. "I heard that one's pretty messed up."

We headed down the corridors, passing the cafeteria just as they let everyone out from breakfast. By the time we reached D-hall, I'd gone over most of the flaws in *Scattered*. And its sequel.

"I mean, yeah, it's got a few good scenes," I told

him. "But the whole virus thing just ruined the ending."

"Yeah, maybe I'll skip that one," said Aaron. "I still want to see *House*, though. And that other one you mentioned, what was it?"

"*Watch the Fog?*" I said.

"Yeah, that one." He glanced up. "Bell's about to ring—I guess I'll see you in band?"

I looked around, startled to realize we were in front of the gym. "Oh! Yeah. See you."

"Bye, Holly." Aaron smiled at me before he disappeared through the double doors. Somehow, I managed to make it to English on time despite the fact that my knees had suddenly decided to go megawobbly.

That was without a doubt the longest conversation I'd ever had with Aaron. I sank down in my chair right as the bell rang, twisting the turtle necklace Julia had given me around my fingers. Maybe I *could* get up the guts to ask him to the dance. I felt my face flush again as I remembered the way he'd smiled at me just now.

Or maybe—just maybe—I wouldn't have to ask him. Maybe he would ask me first.

My good mood lasted all day, despite getting assigned a book report in English, not to mention Mrs. Driscoll springing a pop quiz on us in science. I stayed after school to practice, and I even managed to play the last few measures of the fugue pretty much perfectly five times in a row before walking over to Owen's house.

When I rang his doorbell, I was going over my conversation with Aaron in my head for about the millionth time.

"Hi, Mrs. Grady!" I said cheerfully, holding out an empty Tupperware container. "Thanks again for the brownies last week."

"Anytime, Holly." Mrs. Grady took the container and stepped back to let me in. "How's everything?"

"Great, thanks!" I knelt down to scratch Owen's dog, Worf, behind the ears. "Did Owen tell you about the bake-sale competition we're doing for band?"

She nodded. "He said the brass section is meeting tomorrow morning to get organized."

"Yup." I stood up, brushing stray bits of black and tan fur off my jeans. "Do you think maybe you could help us with the baking? I bet we could sell a ton of those brownies."

Mrs. Grady smiled. "I already promised Owen I'd help. He's in the game room," she added, heading into the kitchen.

"Thank you!" I took the stairs two at a time. Worf raced past me, then stood at the top and watched as I hopped up the last two. "Show-off," I said, and he licked my hand.

"Check it out!"

I'd barely taken two steps into the game room before a sketchbook was shoved inches from my face. It was open to a page with a bloodied Santa Claus ripping a tuba in half. Something pinkish was coming out of the bell of the tuba. I squinted . . . Yeah, it was a brain.

Owen's wide gray eyes peered at me over the top of the book. "What do you think?"

"It's disgusting," I said, then added: "In a good way, I mean. What's it for?"

Owen grinned, leading the way over to the sofa. "The programs for the winter concert. I've been working on some drawings of Mr. Dante in different Santa outfits. That one's zombie Santa, obviously. Here's vampire Santa, and I started a Godzilla Santa, too."

I flipped to the next page, smiling. I'd convinced Mr. Dante to let me make the winter concert programs, since I'd done it last year for Mrs. Wendell. Owen had agreed to draw something for the cover.

"These are stellar," I said. "But the thing is, the winning section gets to pick the costume, and we won't know which section won until right before the concert. We wouldn't have enough time to get them printed."

"Yeah, I know," Owen replied, picking up an orange pencil. "I was thinking we could just have a bunch of different weird Santas on the cover, or something like that." He shrugged, adding flames to the Godzilla Santa's mouth. "What did last year's programs look like? I don't remember."

"They had a big snowflake on the front that I got from clip art," I admitted. Owen's lips twitched. "Hey, I'm not an artist!" I said with a grin. "You're right, a bunch of insane Santas crushing instruments would be a lot cooler. But maybe something with less . . . um . . .

brains. I don't think the band boosters would like that very much."

Owen studied the picture. "Good point."

"Maybe you could do Santa flying a UFO or something," I suggested.

His eyes lit up. "Good idea!" I watched him sit back down with his sketchbook, pencil flying over the paper. It was kind of crazy how fast he could sketch, and how realistic the pictures were.

Well, as realistic as a giant lizard in a Santa hat playing the flute could look.

"Hey, how did you do on that quiz today?" Owen asked. He was my lab partner in science, which was actually how I learned he could draw—he'd made this card game with pictures to help me study because I almost failed the class on my first progress report.

"Aced it," I replied. He smiled, not taking his eyes off the page.

"Nice."

While Owen finished adding a miniature student trying to beat Godzilla Santa away with a drumstick, I went and untangled the video-game controllers lying by the TV. Now that I was passing science, we spent a lot less time studying and a lot more time hijacking alien pods.

"*Prophets* kind of counts as studying science," I realized out loud, flopping back on the sofa. Owen's pencil stopped moving.

"Huh?"

"Think about it—last week I drowned in that lake in level three because I didn't know the aliens could breathe underwater. But they don't have gills. So I bet they breathe through their capillaries, like bullfrogs can."

Owen blinked a few times. "Sometimes you're really weird, Holly." But I could see him smiling as he went back to his sketchbook.

"Thank you."

I tried to get through level four for a few minutes while Owen finished his sketch, then we switched to two-player. Half an hour later, we were battling tree-dwelling aliens in the everglades of level five when Owen's stepfather, Steve, came up the stairs. Owen fumbled with his controller, hastily closing his sketchbook and sliding it under a pile of comic books.

"Dinner's ready. Holly, you're welcome to stay if you like."

"Thanks, Mr. Grady," I replied, glancing curiously at Owen. "That sounds great."

Steve disappeared back downstairs, and Owen stood up. "What?" he said, and I realized I was staring.

"Nothing." I stood, too, and went to turn off the game console. "It just kind of looked like you were hiding your drawings."

Owen shrugged, not meeting my eyes. "Sort of, I guess."

"Why?" I asked. "Does Steve not like them or something?"

"No, he's never really looked at them," Owen said. "Sometimes he gets kind of annoyed when I'm drawing . . . or on the computer, or playing games or whatever. He thinks it's all a waste of time."

I gasped in mock outrage. "*Prophet Wars* is so not a waste of time!"

Owen laughed. "Anyway, he's always trying to get me to go do stuff outside. Last week he took me to a batting cage, where this machine shoots baseballs at you and you practice hitting."

I struggled to keep a straight face as I tried to picture Owen in a batting cage. "And . . . it wasn't fun?"

"It was the most boring and painful hour of my life," Owen replied solemnly, and I snickered. "Hey, are you sure you want to stay for dinner? Mom's been on a health kick lately. Last night we had this soup that was kind of weird. It tasted like grass and medicine."

Shrugging, I headed to the stairs, and he followed. "It's probably better than Chinese takeout for the third time this week—which is what we've got at my house. Hey, Owen?"

He glanced at me. "Yeah?"

"You should show Steve some of your drawings sometime," I told him. "I bet he'd change his mind about it being a waste of time if he saw how good you are."

Owen bent to scoop up Worf, but I saw him blink about a dozen times.

"Yeah, maybe I will sometime."

Chapter Three

Since school started in August, I'd seen some gross things. There was the sixth-grader who ate eleven pieces of pizza on a bet and then puked all over the cafeteria table next to mine. There was the time the B-hall toilets all overflowed and no one knew until the bell rang after second period, and we went out into the hall and started gagging from the smell. There was the time Gabby found ants in her saxophone during band, and there was the science lab where Owen and I dissected an owl "pellet" and found a whole rat skull.

As disgusting as all that was, nothing could compare to the inside of my brother's car.

"I seriously don't get it, Chad." Wrinkling my nose, I brushed potato-chip crumbs off the passenger seat and sat down carefully. I was seriously regretting asking him to take me to the brass section's bake-sale meeting Friday morning. "You've had this car for three weeks. How can it be this nasty already?"

My brother rolled his eyes, knocking a few crumpled soda cans out of the way to buckle his seat belt. "Hey, I woke up half an hour early to help you out. Lay off." His voice was thick and sleepy.

"It's just—oh my *God*." I lifted my feet in the air and stared, horrified, at the giant, gooey brown lump on the carpet. "Do I even want to know what that is?"

Chad squinted, leaning over. "No idea . . . oh man! I bet it's that chocolate bar I bought yesterday. I was wondering what happened to that."

I eyed the brown lump, hugging my knees to my chest. "Are you sure that's what it is?"

Shrugging, Chad checked the rearview mirror and started backing out of our driveway. "Pretty sure."

Ew ew ew. Trying not to breathe in too deeply, I kicked a few empty, grease-stained Chinese-food cartons on top of the brown goop so I wouldn't have to look at it.

Mom and Dad had agreed to get Chad a used car for his birthday last month, but only if he got an after-school job to help pay for half. His friend Toby's uncle happened to be the manager of the Lotus Garden, so he'd hired Chad to do deliveries. At first all the free food had been a bonus, but lately I'd gotten tired of sesame chicken and sweet-and-sour shrimp.

Not the fortune cookies, though. Who could ever get sick of fortune cookies?

I spotted a few crammed into one of the cup holders under the stereo. Hesitating, I pinched the plastic wrapper of the one on top, held it up, and inspected it. It looked safe, but you could never be too careful. After all, the other cup holder was filled with about two inches of what I dearly hoped was Mountain Dew.

"Good idea." Chad grabbed another cookie, ripped off the plastic, and tossed the wrapper in the backseat. "I didn't even have time to grab a cereal bar before we left, thanks to you."

I unwrapped my own cookie and tucked the plastic in my jeans pocket. "It's not my fault. This was the only time everyone could make it." Popping half of the cookie into my mouth, I eagerly unfolded the little slip of paper inside.

BE A GOOD FRIEND AND A FAIR ENEMY

Boring. I stuffed the paper into the front pocket of my backpack and crunched the other half of the cookie. On Tuesday, I'd opened one that said BIG CHANGES IN LOVE ARE AHEAD.

Now *that* was a fortune.

When Chad pulled up in the drop-off lane in front of the main entrance, I opened my door and two soda cans and a Lotus Garden carton fell out on the curb. I glanced around, but thankfully no one was hanging out in the entrance. Shoving the trash back into my brother's mobile garbage can, I grabbed my backpack and hurried to the band hall.

Natasha was there, just pulling open the double doors. "Nice boots," she said with a grin, glancing down at the dark brown boots I was wearing (which happened to be hers).

"Thanks!" I replied. "Nice skirt."

She brushed some imaginary dust off my denim skirt. "You think?"

When Natasha moved here at the beginning of seventh grade, we didn't get along very well at first. Actually, that's putting it nicely. We kind of hated each other. We were always trying to one-up each other in band, and even worse, we were fighting over Julia and putting her in the middle of everything.

It was a good thing we'd managed to get over all that, because Natasha and I had the same taste in clothes. Once we became friends, our wardrobes had doubled.

Since we were a few minutes early for the meeting, there weren't many other kids in the band hall yet. Liam Park was sprawled out over three chairs in the tuba section, one arm over his eyes and the other dangling to the floor. A few chairs down from him, Max Foster was reading a book. Victoria Rios waved at us as she walked out of the cubbies.

Natasha and I joined her, pulling three chairs close together. Victoria yawned widely.

"I can't believe I'm here before eight," she mumbled, rubbing her eyes. "Hey, cool boots," she added, pointing to my feet. "Thanks," Natasha and I said simultaneously.

More kids started to trickle in while we talked, and by eight o'clock, almost the whole brass section was there. I waved to Owen when he walked in with Trevor Wells. Victoria was in the middle of telling us about her track meet yesterday when Aaron came through the doors. I watched him grab a seat next to Liam and shake him awake just as Mr. Dante came out of his office.

"Okay, let's get started," he said, turning one of the chairs in the clarinet section around so he could sit facing us. "I want each section to take care of its own planning, but I'll help you get started. First off, we need a leader to keep track of everything—what you're going to sell, how much you'll charge, who's baking what, all that stuff." Mr. Dante held up a notebook and a pen. "Any volunteers?"

My hands twitched, but I kept them in my lap. I desperately wanted to raise my hand, but the majority of the brass section was eighth-graders. The idea of bossing them all around was kind of intimidating.

Finally, Aaron shrugged and raised his hand. "I'll do it." He took the notebook and pen from Mr. Dante.

My stomach automatically fluttered at the sound of Aaron's voice, but I couldn't help thinking about all the loose papers and books I'd seen falling out of his locker. He might not be too good at the whole organization thing.

Maybe I could offer to help.

Flushed at the thought, I tried to pay attention to Mr. Dante.

"Basically, you can split the responsibilities up any way you like," he was saying. "If someone doesn't want to do the actual baking, they can contribute some other way—wrapping the food and boxing it to take to the games, for example. Or collecting the money to hand in to the band boosters after every game and keeping track of how much you earn. The important thing is that everyone pitches in. If someone isn't pulling their weight, let me know."

Aaron nodded, jotting down notes.

Mr. Dante gave us the dates of the three volleyball tournaments, then got up to head back to his office. "If you have any questions, just ask."

Once his office door was closed, everyone looked at Aaron.

"Okay," he said. "So, um . . . who really doesn't want to bake?"

Victoria's hand shot into the air. Max and Gabe Fernandez raised theirs, too, and after a second, so did Trevor.

Aaron wrote their names down. "Cool. Gabe, how about you take care of collecting all the money and recording how much we make. And the three of you can do the wrapping and boxing. That okay?"

They nodded. After adding that to the notebook, Aaron tapped the pen against his leg. "Okay. So . . . how should we split up the baking?"

"I thought we'd all just make something at home and bring it to the games," said Liam, who still looked half asleep.

"It'd be better to work in groups," said Brooke

Dennis. She was third-chair French horn and sat next to me during rehearsals. "That form Mr. Dante gave us on Monday said we had to have a parent there to supervise with whatever we bake, and my mom works nights. I think the booster parents sent out an e-mail asking for volunteers."

"Oh yeah, I forgot about that." Aaron thought for a minute. "Okay, does anyone know if their parents are planning on volunteering?"

Several students raised their hands, including Owen and Natasha. Aaron jotted their names down. "I'll just split us into groups, and each group can pick whatever day they can meet to bake. Okay?"

While he drew up the group lists, everyone started chatting. "The woodwinds met yesterday after school," Natasha told me and Victoria, picking at a nail. "I think they're working in groups, too."

"Yup—and Julia's dad volunteered," I said. "He's going to help them make those s'mores cupcakes Julia brought to your birthday party."

Natasha groaned. "Those are so good. We're doomed." I nodded glumly in agreement. Mr. Gordon had never made anything that wasn't ridiculously delicious.

"Not to worry, girls," Victoria said with a grin. "Know who else's mom volunteered for the woodwinds?"

I thought for a second, then grinned. "Gabby's?"

Victoria nodded emphatically. "She said her mom's making some sort of fake cheesecake with tofu or something. Gabby was talking about hiding it under the bleachers."

Natasha and I laughed. Gabby's mom was kind of crazy when it came to eating healthy, which was why Gabby was constantly snacking on Red Hots and M&M's during class. She had to make up for all the wheatgrass juice and beet casserole.

Mr. Dante came out of his office and started rummaging through the folder on his podium. "Don't mind me," he said mildly. Liam spoke up, looking slightly more alert now.

"Mr. Dante, when you said the winning section could pick our shirt designs, did you mean we could actually design them ourselves?"

Straightening up, Mr. Dante frowned thoughtfully. "Well, the company I've chosen has hundreds of designs—I was thinking you'd just choose from those. But they *can* do custom designs, so maybe . . ." He stopped, raising an eyebrow. "Can any of you draw?"

"Owen!" It burst out before I could stop myself. "He's really, really good, you guys. I swear."

"It's true, he's an awesome artist," Natasha chimed in, right at the same time that Trevor said, "Definitely."

Owen looked half pleased, half like he wanted to crawl under his chair and die. I smiled at him encouragingly.

"Well, I think it would be pretty cool to have custom-designed shirts." Mr. Dante closed his folder, sheet music in hand. "Of course, you have to win first," he added with a grin.

"Are you sure you want us to?" Aaron asked. "Because we really like that Mrs. Claus idea."

Everyone laughed, but Mr. Dante just smiled. "I'm sure I could pull it off," he said before heading back into his office.

When the bell rang, Natasha jumped to her feet. "I forgot I have to stop at my locker before history," she said quickly. "Want to walk with me?"

I glanced at Aaron, who was still writing down a few notes. "Nah, I need to get something out of my cubby. See you at lunch!"

"See you!" Natasha hurried out of the band hall, along with almost everyone else. Ignoring the butterflies swooping around in my stomach, I followed Aaron when he stood and walked into the cubbies.

"Let me know if you need any help with all this," I said as casually as possible, pretending to look for something in my cubby. "I'm pretty good at organizational stuff."

"Really?" Aaron said as he unzipped his backpack and stuffed the notebook inside. "That'd be great, because I'm kind of . . . not."

No kidding, I thought, staring at the inside of his bag. With all the loose papers in there, I wondered why he even bothered buying folders.

"Hey, do you have any of those *Watch the Fog* movies on DVD?"

"Yeah, I've got all of them!" I said. (Okay, so technically they were Chad's, but Aaron didn't need to know that.)

"Would it be cool if I borrowed them sometime?" he asked as we walked out of the band hall together. "Or maybe just the first one."

"Sure!" I spotted Julia at her locker and waved. "I'll bring them next week. Are you going to your locker?"

"Nah, I've got everything." Aaron grinned at me. "Thanks, Holly! See you."

"See you."

He disappeared around the corner, and I walked over to Julia. Or maybe floated was a better word. She snickered, closing her locker.

"So what was *that* about?"

"Nothing," I said, trying not to smile (and failing). "He asked to borrow a movie. And I offered to help him organize our bake sale—he volunteered to be in charge."

Julia quirked an eyebrow. "Good thing he's got you, then. I've seen the inside of his locker. And apparently his English teacher told him she'd give him bonus points if he ever turned in a paper that didn't look like it'd been shoved in his pockets for days."

I laughed. "How do you know that?"

"Natasha," Julia said, slinging her backpack on her shoulder. "She's got debate last period right across the hall from his English class, so I guess they see each other after school sometimes."

"Oh," I said. *Weird that Natasha never mentioned that to me.*

"Anyway . . ." Julia cleared her throat just as the warning bell rang. "So you're helping him with the fund-raiser, walking to class together, he even has the same creeptastical taste in movies as you . . . maybe you won't have to go through with our pact, huh? I bet he asks you first!"

I grinned, the butterflies back in full force. "Yeah, maybe."

Chapter Four

I practiced Fugue in F Minor so much on Saturday that by Sunday morning, even Chad was humming it under his breath. (Until he realized what he was doing. Then he threw a piece of toast at me and told Mom he was soundproofing his room.) So I decided to give them all a break from my practicing, and invited Julia and Natasha over instead.

"I brought a movie," Julia said as we entered my room, pulling a DVD out of her purse and waving it in front of my face. I read the title and groaned. "*The Lost Journal?* Are you kidding me?"

"You owe us, Holly." Julia marched straight to my TV and pulled the DVD out of its case. "Consider this haunted-house payback."

Nodding fervently in agreement, Natasha grabbed a pillow from my bed and sprawled out on the floor. "For real. I'm still having nightmares about those clowns."

I rolled my eyes. "They weren't that scary."

"They didn't have teeth!" Natasha cried.

"Exactly!" I said. "Even if one had caught you, it couldn't bite you. I mean, it *could*, but it's not like it would've hurt—" I stopped, because Natasha had buried her head under the pillow with a muffled scream.

Julia giggled, nudging Natasha with her toe. "Give it up," she told her. "Holly and I have had this argument a billion times." She pressed PLAY, then sat on the floor and leaned against my bed. Soft orchestral music began drifting out of the speakers, and the words *The Lost Journal* appeared on the screen in fancy script. "Here you go, Holly," she added with a grin, tossing me a package of tissues. "You're going to need these."

As if.

Two hours later, Natasha was weeping into my pillow and Julia was blowing her nose for probably the hundredth time. When the closing credits started to roll, she turned and said something to me.

"Huh?" Lowering my book, I pulled the earphones out of my ears.

"You didn't even watch it!" Julia said accusingly, rubbing her eyes.

"I watched the first twenty minutes, which was payback enough." I set the book on my night table and stretched. "*Believe* me."

Natasha sat up, grabbing for a tissue. Her face was red and blotchy. "You should've watched the whole thing," she said, her voice muffled as she wiped her nose. "If you'd seen the ending . . ."

"I don't have to see the ending," I told her. "I know what happens. She dies. His heart's broken but he patches things up with his family and becomes a better person. The end."

Natasha's eyes widened. "How did you know?"

"Oh, please," I said, rolling my eyes. "It was obvious from the beginning."

Julia laughed despite herself. "It's no use," she said to Natasha. "I've made Holly watch almost all of my favorite movies. She always knows the ending before it's even halfway finished."

"I'll tell you what a better ending would've been." I grabbed my remote, muting the obnoxious sappy music. "If she'd possessed that journal after she died, then she could hypnotize whoever read it like in *Dark Omnibus,* then *he* would've been possessed when he found the journal right after her funeral, and—"

A pillow to the head stopped me from finishing.

"Fine!" I yelled. "No more horror-movie talk. Even if they are a zillion times better."

"Good," said Julia. "So, any idea what you guys are making for the volleyball game on Thursday? I heard the brass section split into groups, like we did. I'm not on baking duty till the last game."

"I'm in the second group," I said. "Natasha's in the one for this week though, right?"

Aaron had given us all a list of the three groups he'd split us into after band on Friday. I was more than a little bummed that he hadn't put us in the same group.

He was in the first one, too.

"We're meeting at Liam's house after school Wednesday," Natasha told us. "I think Liam said something about homemade doughnuts—I guess his dad makes them a lot. And we're making cookies and brownies . . . typical stuff."

"Don't even tell us what your dad's planning on doing," I said to Julia. "We already know about the s'mores cupcakes."

"Okay," she said with a rather evil grin. "I won't tell you about the chocolate banana bread. Or the pumpkin streusel muffins, or the cinnamon mini scones, or the—"

"Yeah," I interrupted. "We're dead." Natasha nodded sadly, and Julia giggled.

"Sorry, guys," she said. "This is kind of a cool fundraiser, though. Better than just selling those plants, like we did in beginner band. And the orchestra is doing a raffle, which is kind of boring."

Natasha and I shared a knowing glance. Seth Anderson played cello in the school's orchestra.

"They are?" I asked innocently. "I didn't know that. What are the prizes?"

Julia was busy putting her DVD back in its case. "Um . . . tickets to Splash Park, some gift cards, I think maybe an iPod . . ."

Natasha cleared her throat. "So how many tickets did you buy?"

"Just five," Julia said, then caught herself. She made

a face as Natasha and I burst out laughing.

"So is Seth returning the favor?" I asked between giggles. "He'd better be at the game Thursday, and he'd better buy at least five cupcakes."

"Actually, he probably will be there," Julia admitted, her cheeks still flushed. "His sister's on the volleyball team."

"How convenient." Natasha propped a pillow up and leaned against the wall. "Seriously, Julia. How long are you going to wait before you just tell him you like him?"

Julia glanced at me. "Well . . . actually, I've decided to ask him to the winter dance in a few weeks."

Natasha sat up straight. "Are you really?" she squealed. "Wait—why a few weeks? Why not now?"

I realized suddenly that Julia hadn't filled Natasha in on our pact. And as much as I loved Natasha, I still felt a little weird talking about Aaron with her. Back when we were enemies, she'd intentionally flirted with him at the band party just to upset me. She apologized for it and I totally forgave her, but it was sort of an awkward subject.

"Because I made her promise the other day that if Seth didn't ask her to the dance by Thanksgiving break, she'd ask him," I told Natasha quickly. "He likes her— he's just too shy to ask. Don't you think?"

"*Yes.*" Natasha beamed at Julia. "This is so cool! What are you going to wear?"

Julia was laughing. "You guys are acting like we're already going together!"

"If you ask him, he'll say yes," I said firmly. Natasha nodded in agreement.

"We'll see, I guess." Julia smiled, shaking her head. "What about you?" she asked, nudging Natasha with her foot. "Is there anyone you're thinking about asking?"

Natasha shrugged. "Not really."

"What about that guy on the debate team?" I said. "What's-his-name, the really cute one you were talking to after lunch a few weeks ago."

"Oh, that's Brian Sanders," she replied, suddenly very interested in the back of Julia's DVD case. "Yeah, he's cute. Really nice, too."

It wasn't like Natasha to be so evasive. Apparently, Julia was thinking the same thing, since she reached forward and yanked the case out of Natasha's hands.

"Do you like him?" Julia asked eagerly. "Come on, spill. I deserve to know after all the teasing I get about Seth. And Holly, too, about Aaron," she added. "Like last week with Gabby and the folder, remember?"

I groaned. Gabby was constantly pushing me to just tell Aaron I liked him. Last week she'd taped a piece of pink construction paper on the inside of my band folder that said I <3 U AARON COOK. Mr. Dante asked us to take out our warm-up chorale, I'd opened my folder, and there it was, right where Aaron could see from his chair behind me. Luckily, I'd slammed it shut before anyone (other than Natasha or Gabby) saw a thing.

"It wasn't funny," I protested, because Julia was giggling again. "Just because it's easy for Gabby to talk to guys, she thinks it should be easy for everyone."

"Hey, did you hear Max asked her to the dance already?" Natasha said. "Sophie told me Friday after school. And she said Brooke and Gabe are going together, too." If there were all-region auditions for gossip, Sophie Wheeler would be first chair.

"Gabby and Max?" I said, surprised. "She's never mentioned liking him before."

Natasha started to respond, but was cut off by my mom calling up the stairs.

"Girls, Mr. Gordon's here!"

As Julia and Natasha put their shoes on, I grabbed *The Lost Journal* and held it out like a smelly sock. "Don't forget this, please."

Julia laughed, sticking the DVD in her purse. We headed downstairs, and Natasha and I waved from the doorway as Julia jumped into the front seat of her dad's truck. As soon as he pulled out of the driveway, Mrs. Prynne's car pulled up. I turned to Natasha.

"If you like him, you should tell him."

Natasha's eyes widened. "What?"

"Brian!" I said. "Seriously, if you like him, you should just tell him. Ask him to the dance or something!"

"Oh!" Natasha smiled, but it seemed a bit forced. "I don't know . . ."

"I know it's scary, but I bet if you ask him, he'll say yes." I gave her an encouraging smile. "*If* you like him, I mean."

Mrs. Prynne beeped her horn, and Natasha gave me a quick hug.

"I'll think about it. Thanks, Holly!"

I waved as their car pulled away, then headed upstairs to my brother's room and knocked on the door.

"Yeah?"

I opened the door and stepped inside. Or, more accurately, I kicked aside an empty box of crackers and stepped over a small mountain of dirty laundry. Chad was in front of his TV, game controller in hand, eyes glazed over. I watched the screen as his character launched himself off a building onto a helicopter, which swerved. He'd nearly made it inside when the pilot kicked him in the shoulder. The character plummeted to the ground and the screen faded to black. Chad glared at me.

"That was your fault."

"Yeah right." I headed over to his movie shelf. "You should get *Prophet Wars*. It's a lot better than that game."

Chad glanced at me in surprise. "Yeah, I played *Prophets* once. Toby's got it. How do you even know about it?"

"I rock that game."

Chad snorted loudly. "Sure you do."

"I do," I said matter-of-factly, searching the shelf and silently wishing Chad would just let me alphabetize it already. After all, I watched these movies just as much as he did—several of them were mine—and it was so hard to find anything. I spotted *Watch the Fog 2* stuck between the original version of *Carrie* and one of those old Nightmare on Elm Street slasher movies. Seriously, even the sequels weren't shelved together. It made my palms itchy just looking at it.

A tinny explosion sound from the TV speakers told me Chad had restarted his game. "What are you looking for, anyway?" he asked without looking away from the screen.

"I need to borrow *Watch the Fog*. All three of them, actually." I slid *Watch the Fog 2* off the shelf, then stared at *Carrie*, chewing my lip. "Would it really be so hard to keep these organized? If you'd just let me—"

"Nope," Chad cut me off. "The first one's over there on my dresser. Leon's got the third one."

I hesitated a moment, then took the *Carrie* DVD, too. Crossing the room, I grabbed the *Watch the Fog* case, along with two of the fortune cookies scattered across the dresser. "Thanks."

"Sure. You going to watch them right now?"

"No, I'm lending them to . . . someone."

Chad paused his game to look at me. "Who? Not Julia or what's-her-name. I thought they were gonna pass out in the Asylum."

"Her name's Natasha, and no way, it's not for them," I said, edging toward the door.

"Who then?"

"Just a . . . friend," I replied. "This guy."

Chad squinted. "What guy?"

Rolling my eyes, I back-stepped over the dirty

laundry. "Just a guy, that's all."

"What's his name?"

"Aaron."

"He's in your class?"

Oh, great. "No, eighth grade," I said, then sighed when Chad adopted an expression of mock concern.

"Oh, I don't know, Holly. I don't think I want you using my DVDs to flirt with guys. Especially *older* guys."

"I'm not flirting!" I protested, probably a little too quickly. "I mean, this isn't . . . we're just . . . I don't even . . ."

"Don't even what?"

I groaned as Dad stepped into Chad's room, making a face as he kicked a few empty Chinese take-out cartons aside.

"Holly's lending my movies to her boyfriend, that's what," Chad said, snickering when I shot him a death glare. Dad glanced at the DVDs in my hand, eyebrows raised.

"Boyfriend?"

"He's not—" I started, right as Chad said: "He's in eighth grade."

"Really?" Dad nodded slowly, rubbing his chin. "Interesting."

"He's *not* my boyfriend," I said, my face burning. "He's just this guy in band."

"The one whose house you go to every Thursday?" Dad asked.

"Well . . . no."

"Hmm." Dad exchanged an amused look with Chad, and I edged toward the door. "Maybe we need to meet this guy."

"No, you really, *really* don't."

"Oh, come on, Holly," Chad said, grinning. "Invite him over for dinner. We could—"

He stopped, because I'd lobbed one of the fortune cookies at him. I stayed just long enough to watch it bounce off his forehead before I ran out of his room, slamming the door behind me.

Back in the safety of my bedroom, I slid all three movies into my backpack, then grabbed my book and flopped down on my bed. But instead of opening the book, I set it on my stomach and ripped the plastic off the fortune cookie. The slip of paper was already sticking out of one end. I unfolded it, popped the entire cookie in my mouth, and promptly choked.

YOUR SECRET ADMIRER WILL SOON BE REVEALED

The logical part of me knew fortune cookies were meaningless, along with horoscopes, palm readings, and Ouija boards. But that didn't stop me from squeaking like a clarinet with a broken reed and doing a happy dance that knocked most of the smaller pillows off my bed.

Briefly, I wondered if I should laminate this little fortune. Then I realized I was being ridiculous. I would just fold it up and carry it like a good luck charm in my pocket tomorrow for when I saw Aaron.

If you like him, you should tell him. That's what I'd said to Natasha about Brian. And that's what we kept telling Julia about Seth. Maybe it was about time I took my own advice. If my best friends could ask their crushes to the dance, I should be able to ask Aaron, too.

Sighing, I gazed at the fortune. Even if my secret admirer *was* ready to reveal himself, I just might beat him to it.

Chapter Five

I changed clothes about five times Monday morning before settling on a flared-sleeve top with a wavy turquoise pattern that Mom said brought out my eyes, white capris, and a blue headband. I knew I'd be paying for it later when I had to rearrange my whole week's worth of outfits, but whatever. If today was the day my "secret admirer" would be revealed, well then, I was going to look good.

The fortune was rolled up neatly inside my front right pocket, but I kept pulling it out and reading it on my way to first-period English.

"What's that?" Gabby asked around a mouthful of M&M's (her typical breakfast).

"Nothing," I said hastily, cramming the fortune back into my pocket and plopping down at my desk. "Hey, so you're going to the winter dance with Max?"

Gabby picked out five yellow M&M's and handed them to me. "Nope. He asked, but I said no."

I winced, popping the candy into my mouth. "That must've been awkward."

She shrugged. "Not really. We're just friends—he lives on my street. He's had a huge crush on Christine Pope forever, but she's got a boyfriend."

"Oh," I said, but privately I was thinking saying no to a friend asking you for a date had to be even more awkward than turning down some guy you barely knew.

Having gym right before band so did not help my nerves. It's hard to feel confident when you're all sweaty and your hair has the kind of frizz that comes with doing sprints outside in humid weather. But when I got to the band hall early (and admittedly a little out of breath) and saw Aaron alone at his cubby, I told myself to get over it. *No excuses.*

Patting my hair down for the billionth time, I headed to my cubby and slid my case out. "Hi, Aaron!"

"Hey, Holly," he said, closing the notebook Mr. Dante had given him. "How's it going?"

"Good." I unzipped my backpack and pulled out the DVDs. "Here you go. Sorry it's just the first two. My brother, um . . . borrowed the third one from me."

Aaron's eyes widened in surprise. "Oh, cool!" He flipped one of them over and read the back, then shot me a grin that made my legs feel like Jell-O. "Thanks, Holly. I'll check them out this week."

"You're welcome." My voice sounded a little higher than normal, but he didn't seem to notice. I took my time getting out my horn while he read the back of the other DVD. More kids were trickling in now, including Julia and Natasha. I waved, and Julia glanced pointedly at Aaron and gave me a little thumbs-up. Stifling a giggle, I turned around and knelt down by my backpack.

Okay, here we go. I'd rehearsed this carefully in my head all night.

"So I brought this one, too, if you're interested," I said, straightening up and holding out another DVD. Aaron took it and scanned the title.

"*Carrie* . . . definitely heard of it, never seen it," he said. "But I remember seeing the poster at that theater downtown that only shows old horror movies."

"Horror Hall," I said immediately. "That's where I saw *The Exorcist* for the first time."

Aaron gestured to the *Carrie* case. "Isn't this the one where the girl goes nuts and burns down her school or something?"

"Yeah, she's telekinetic," I explained. "Everyone's really horrible to her, so she gets revenge at the school dance by . . ."

I stopped, even though my brain was screaming *Keep talking! Talk about the dance!* But my voice would not cooperate. It was like my vocal cords were suddenly frozen or something.

"Actually, I think I've seen parts of this!" Aaron was examining the pictures on the back of the case. "Not the whole thing, though. I'll check it out." He flipped the case over to the front, which showed Carrie in her prom-queen crown, covered in pig's blood. He grinned at me. Ugh, stupid weak knees. "Too bad we don't have a Halloween dance, huh? This would be a killer costume."

Somehow I managed to answer, despite the sudden buzzing in my ears. "Yeah. Well, I could dress like Carrie for the winter dance. Really freak everybody out."

Aaron laughed, then glanced over my shoulder. "Hey, speaking of . . . can I ask you something?"

Oh my God.

Nod head. Use vocal cords. "Sure!" I squeaked.

"What's that?"

Dazed, I watched as Liam took one of the *Watch the Fog* movies from Aaron. "Oh yeah, I heard this is awesome," he said enthusiastically, glancing at the other DVDs. "These yours?"

"Nah, Holly's letting me borrow them," Aaron said. I smiled weakly at Liam, when really I wanted to say *Seriously? Seriously, you had to walk up right when Aaron was about to—*

The bell rang, cutting off my mental rant. I watched Aaron head into the band hall with Liam, disappointment settling in. Reaching into my front pocket, I touched the fortune and my stomach swooped.

So we'd been interrupted. That wasn't important, really. I grabbed my horn, replaying the last few seconds of our conversation over and over again in my head until I was convinced I was right.

Aaron had been about to ask me to the dance. All I had to do was make sure he had another opportunity.

𝄞

Trying to have a private conversation in middle school is totally impossible.

Despite my best efforts all week, by Thursday I still hadn't gotten to talk to Aaron again. I mean, other than just saying hi in passing. He wasn't in the band hall in the mornings, and the cubbies were always annoyingly crowded right before rehearsal.

But I wasn't giving up hope. Thursday night was the first volleyball tournament, and I was going to do my best to talk to him then. That turned out to be easier said than done in a gym crowded with coaches, volleyball players, and cheering parents from two different schools.

I spotted Victoria, Natasha, and Liam in the parking lot, taking foil-covered platters and stacks of Tupperware out of the trunk of Mrs. Park's car. Natasha waved me over.

"This is everything we made last night," she told me. "It's a zoo in there—there are two games going on, one in each gym. I think we're going to split up to try to sell as much as we can during both games."

It didn't take long to realize that I wasn't going to get a chance to talk to Aaron, at least not until after the tournament. Just like Natasha said, half the band ended up in one gym and half in the other. And while I was in the auxiliary gym with Aaron, we were working at tables on opposite sides. I couldn't help feeling a twinge of jealousy that Natasha happened to be over there with him, working side-by-side. It wasn't her fault, though—a few of the band boosters had taken charge and assigned us all spots.

Owen and Victoria were at my table, though, so it wasn't like I had no one to talk to. Not that we had much of a chance to talk. It was hard to hear with all the cheering and the squeaks of tennis shoes on the gym floor. Plus, the constant line at our table seemed to triple during breaks in the game. Twice Owen and I had to run back out to Mrs. Park's car to bring in more desserts.

"This is fun, kind of," I said, blowing a strand of hair out of my eyes and struggling under the weight of four trays of cookies.

"Kind of," Owen agreed, balancing a stack of brownie-filled containers. "Not as much fun as *Prophets*, though. I'm glad the next two tournaments aren't on Thursdays."

I nodded. "We'll make up for it tomorrow after school. Alien marathon."

Every time I had a few seconds to spare, I jotted down exactly what we sold in my own little notebook. The peanut butter cookie sandwiches seemed to be the most popular, while the lemon bars were the least. I figured I'd let Aaron know which items sold the best so we could include more of them at the next two games.

"How much longer?" Victoria asked Mrs. Park when she came to check on us. She squinted at the scoreboard.

"Hard to say . . . There's another match after this one, so at least an hour, I'd guess."

"Look, guys, there's no one in line," I pointed out. "Let's get the table filled up while we can."

For a few minutes, no one spoke as we stacked and organized almost everything we had left to sell on the table. When we finished, Victoria wiped her brow.

"Maybe it would've been easier to just sell plants," she muttered.

"Yeah, but we wouldn't make nearly as much money," said Gabe Fernandez, who was standing next to Max at the end of the table. He tapped the metal box we were keeping the cash in. "We've already made almost two hundred dollars, just at this table."

"Wow," I said, glancing around the gym. "I wonder how the other sections are doing." The woodwinds had two tables in this gym and two in the other, just like we did, and the percussionists had one table in each. I glanced over at the other brass table, where Aaron was taking money from a little girl who was standing on tiptoes, choosing a cookie. She headed back up the bleachers, and Aaron turned and started talking to Natasha.

"Here comes Trevor," Owen said. I tore my eyes away from Aaron and saw Trevor leaving their table and heading our way, keeping close to the walls.

"Do you guys have any of those brownies left?" he asked when he reached us. "We're sold out."

"Yeah, I think we have some under here." I

ducked down under the table and grabbed the last two containers of brownies. Overhead, I heard Gabe yell, "Look out!" and a few gasps from the crowd.

I straightened up just in time to see Trevor spin around. The game seemed to be on pause for a split second; the girls on both teams were all staring at our table. I barely had time to wonder why when the volleyball smacked a surprised Trevor square in the chest.

He staggered back, arms helicoptering at his sides in a way that almost would've been funny. Almost, except when he finally lost his balance and fell backward, he fell on our table. And that was not funny at all.

Everyone leaped back as the flimsy table legs gave out. With a loud *crunch*, the table collapsed with Trevor on top, sprawled flat on his back with a tray of smashed cookies sticking out from under his elbow and a halo of purple cupcake frosting around his head.

"Trevor!" I gasped. Everyone crowded around, squashing brownies and kicking trays aside, to help pull him up.

"Are you okay?"

"Are you hurt?"

"Dude, that was pretty wicked looking."

"I'm fine," Trevor mumbled, rubbing his shoulder and stumbling away from the wrecked table. His face was a dull red. Now that he was on his feet and surrounded by parents, the game resumed. I heard laughter coming from the bleachers and gave the group of eighth-graders pointing and snickering at Trevor my best death glare. *Seriously? Grow up.*

Mrs. Park and a few other parents led Trevor out of the gym, and the rest of us stared at the mess on the floor.

"Well, let's clean this up," Victoria decided. "Maybe if our other tables have extras, we can try to sell them."

"I don't know . . . Trevor said they were already out of brownies," Gabe said glumly, leaning over to pick up the metal cash box and brushing off a smashed lemon bar. "We just lost a lot of money."

I saw Aaron, Natasha, and the others looking at us from across the gym, and I could tell they were thinking the same thing.

It was going to be next to impossible to raise enough money to win now.

Chapter Six

"**Y**ou look like you need these."

Gabby shook a bag of M&M's at me as soon as I walked into English on Friday morning. I reached out for a handful, but she dropped the whole thing into my hands.

"I brought two," she said, showing me her own bag. "Sorry about what happened at the game last night."

"Thanks." I ripped it open and shoved a handful of candy into my mouth. The brass section had been the last to leave last night—it took a while to clean up the mess from Trevor's accident. And I barely got to speak two words to Aaron the whole time.

"It's going to be hard for us to catch up now," I said. "Do you know how much the woodwinds made yesterday?"

Gabby shrugged. "Not exactly, but we sold everything we made at both tables. Sorry," she added when I made a face.

"It's okay," I said. "I'm just frustrated about . . . other stuff."

Gabby paused with a handful of M&M's in front of her mouth. "You mean Aaron stuff?"

Now it was my turn to shrug. "Yeah. It's no big deal, though."

"Totally." For some reason, Gabby looked relieved. "I know you'll find another date. Or hey—you can go stag, like me!"

I blinked in confusion. "What are you talking about?"

She froze, then gave me the side-eye. "Um . . . nothing. What are *you* talking about?"

"Gabby!"

Sighing, Gabby leaned closer. "Okay, here's the deal. I was talking to Sophie last night after the tournament, and she said she overheard Aaron talking to Liam. About the dance."

At the sympathetic look on her face, I swallowed a few M&M's whole. They slid down my throat like little pebbles. "And?"

"Well . . ." Gabby hesitated, then blurted it out fast. "Sophie said Liam said, 'Did you ask her yet?' and Aaron said he was about to but got interrupted. Or something like that. I mean, the point is . . ." She paused, chewing her lip. "It sounds like Aaron likes someone, and he's going to ask her to the dance. I'm really, *really* sorry."

I sat there, playing what she'd said on repeat in my head. A slow tingle started in my stomach. "Gabby, I think . . . I think it's me."

She raised an eyebrow. "What?"

My heart was hammering in my ears. "The other day before band I was talking to Aaron and I brought up the dance, and he said, 'Can I ask you something?' but then Liam *interrupted* us. Aaron was talking about me—he's going to ask me to the dance!"

Gabby's mouth fell open. "Awesome!" she cried, and several students turned to stare at us. I tried to hush her, but it was difficult when I couldn't stop giggling.

Leaning back in her chair, Gabby beamed at me. "And this whole time I've been so worried about telling you that he liked someone! Although I'm kind of bummed you won't be going without a date. We'd have fun." Tilting her head, she poured the last few M&M's into her mouth.

I grinned. "Yeah, that would definitely be fun. But hey, someone else might ask you."

"Mike Andrews already has."

"Oh!" I said. Mike was in computer lab with me and Julia. "That's great!"

"I said no." Catching the look on my face, Gabby laughed. "What?"

"What do you mean, what?" I exclaimed. "Why do you keep turning down dates with all these guys?"

"Because I don't want a date at all," Gabby replied matter-of-factly. "My cousin Elena is a senior, right? So last year this guy she liked asked her to prom, and she said yes. But that was, like, a month before prom. They hung out a few times and she said it turned out he was kind of annoying. By the time prom came along, she didn't like him anymore, but they'd already bought the tickets and gotten a limo and all that." Pulling out her notebook when Mr. Franks walked in, Gabby lowered her voice. "So the homecoming dance was a few weeks ago, and Elena just went with a group of girlfriends instead of a date. She said it was way more fun, because a bunch of guys went without dates, too, so she got to dance with a lot of them instead of just one." Gabby grinned. "Sounds like a good deal to me."

I laughed. "Yeah, that makes sense."

And it sort of did, actually. But there was only one boy I planned on dancing with at the winter dance. I turned to face the front as Mr. Franks started taking roll. Focusing on classes was going to be kind of hard today.

Aaron was already in his chair talking to a few other trumpet players by the time I got to band. And I didn't get a chance to talk to him after class either, because he was too busy chatting with Liam and Gabe. It kind of bothered me. It's not like I expected him to just ask me right in the middle of rehearsal or anything, but other than "Hey, Holly!" he didn't say much to me at all.

If he wanted to ask me to the dance, why didn't he just do it already?

At lunch, Julia filled us in on the fund-raiser results. "Melanie told us we totaled over eight hundred dollars," she said, unwrapping a package of cookies. "And I found out from Leah that the percussion section made almost six hundred dollars, but there's only seven of them, so they've got a higher average per student than us. And you guys," she added sympathetically.

"Wow, how did they make so much money?" I asked.

"They made caramel popcorn," Natasha replied. "I went over to their table to see why their line was so long. Everyone loved it, plus it's easy to make so they had a ton of it."

They kept talking, but my eyes kept sliding over to Aaron's table. He always ate with his football friends— the thought of going over there with all of those guys around terrified me. Nope, no way I'd ever be able to ask him to the dance during lunch. I glanced at him again, and my stomach flip-flopped when I saw him looking my direction.

All of a sudden, I didn't know what to do with my hands. I put down my sandwich, picked it up, put it down again, then flipped my hair over my shoulder and tried to look like I was listening to Julia. I kept myself turned so that I could see him out of the corner of my eye.

He was still looking.

"Oh no," Natasha said suddenly. "I left my Spanish book in the band hall." She stood quickly, glanced at the clock, and crumpled her paper bag into a ball. "I'm going to run and get it before the bell rings. See you guys!"

"Bye!" Julia called after her, then she turned and gave me an expectant look. "Okay, what's going on? You look like you're going to bust!"

I bounced up and down on the bench next to her. "Aaron's going to ask me to the dance," I said in a voice that was supposed to be hushed but came out kind of like a shouted whisper.

Her eyes widened. "Are you serious? How do you know?"

I filled her in on everything Gabby told me. By the time I finished, Julia was beaming.

"I'm not surprised, though," she said right as the bell rang. We both stood up and headed for the trash cans.

"Why?"

Julia looked pointedly over at Aaron's table. "I'm not blind, Holly. He spent, like, the whole lunch period staring over here."

I pretty much floated to science class.

After school, I met Owen right outside the band hall and we walked to his house together to make up for the *Prophets* time we lost thanks to the volleyball game. Mrs. Driscoll had handed out a whole bunch of papers about the science fair today in class. The fair wasn't until May, but Owen already couldn't stop talking about it. Actually, it was the grand prize he couldn't stop talking about—a private tour of the NASA Space Center in Houston.

Okay, even I had to admit that was pretty cool.

"You can watch astronauts—*real* ones—training to go to the space station," Owen was saying, reading one of the brochures Mrs. Driscoll had given us as we walked. "And there's a rocket simulation! And—oh, wow, Holly, we could actually see *Gemini V*, like the actual one that went into space, and . . ."

He was like that pretty much the whole walk, tripping over his own feet every other minute because he couldn't take his eyes off the brochure. Then again, I probably didn't look any less goofy. I couldn't stop thinking about Aaron, I couldn't stop smiling, and my fingers kept grazing the secret-admirer fortune in my pocket.

I hadn't seen Aaron for the rest of the day, but then again, I usually didn't—his classes were nowhere near mine. But I wasn't too disappointed. Not when I had actual proof he liked me. *Thank you, Sophie Wheeler, for being so wonderfully nosy.*

When we got to his house, Owen finally put all the science fair stuff away. Since we didn't have any science homework, we blew up alien pods for a solid two hours.

"Level eight!" I yelled triumphantly, tossing my controller down and rubbing my eyes. "Ow. I think I need a break."

"Me too." Owen stood up and stretched. "Want a drink?"

"Sure."

We headed downstairs to the kitchen and found Worf with his head in the trash can.

"Hey!" Owen cried, pulling him out. Worf clutched a soggy paper towel in his teeth, tail wagging furiously. "Mom, Worf's in the trash again!"

"Well, get him out!" Mrs. Grady called from her office. "And Owen, don't ruin your dinner—I'm ordering pizza in a few minutes."

"Can Holly stay?"

"Of course!"

"If you want," Owen added, picking up the trash on the floor and throwing it away. "We could put in *Cyborgs*."

"Only if you're ready to lose," I said with a grin. At the beginning of the year, Owen had bet that I couldn't guess the ending of his favorite movie, *Cyborgs versus Ninjas*. (Yeah, right.)

Owen was laughing. "If you say so. We can probably watch about half before the pizza gets here."

"Okay! I just have to call my dad—he's supposed to pick me up." I watched Worf bat an empty soup can around the kitchen floor. "Pizza, huh? What happened to your mom's diet?"

Owen glanced in the direction of his mom's office and lowered his voice. "No diet on the weekends."

"Why?"

He shrugged, getting a bottle of soda out of the fridge. "Dunno. Last Saturday we grilled burgers, and Sunday morning she bought a giant box of doughnuts. But then Monday she got all strict again and made this massive salad for dinner. It's like on Mondays she hits the diet-reboot button."

"Weird."

Owen handed me a glass of soda, then pushed himself up to sit on the edge of the counter. "So, got any ideas for our science fair project?"

I groaned. "*Owen.* It's not until May!"

"Yeah, but we're supposed to start working on them right after winter break!" Owen said. "Besides, I thought you'd be into this."

"Why?" I asked. "I do okay in science now, but it's not exactly my favorite subject."

"Yeah, but come on, Holly." Owen grinned at me. "The fair's a *competition.* A big one, too. The whole school district."

He had a point.

"Okay," I said. "Is there a theme or something?"

"Life," Owen said simply. "It's pretty open. We could do something on plant life, or animal life—we can't use live animals, though, or—"

"Aliens," I interrupted. "Could we do one on alien life?"

He laughed. "Seriously?"

"Why not?" I said, warming to the thought. "Like what kind of alien could live on Venus or something. Or what you'd need to build a city on Mars! We could ask Mrs. Driscoll, at least."

"Okay!" Owen looked excited. "Maybe we could even get started on it before winter break."

"Sure!" I said. Worf finally settled down at my feet,

chewing on a shoelace. "It might be hard to find time, though. Thanksgiving's the week after next, then all-region, the winter dance, the concert, and that's the end of the semester."

"Yeah, true."

It suddenly occurred to me that I'd just spent my entire Friday afternoon playing video games, and now I was planning a science project six months in advance. *What a geek*, I thought, sipping my drink. But it didn't really bother me. Maybe being a geek was cool.

"Holly, would you go to the dance with me?" Owen said suddenly. I spit out a mouthful of soda and sent Worf into another frenzy.

"What?" I wasn't entirely positive I'd heard him right.

Owen's eyes went wide with alarm, and he held his hands out like a crossing guard. *Stop.*

"No, I don't mean, you know, like a date or anything!" he said hastily. "I meant just as friends. Just friends. If you want to. I thought it'd be fun."

Grabbing the paper towels, I wondered which one of us had the redder face. "Oh! Yeah, that *would* be fun!" My voice came out all weird and high and loud, like a cheerleader on a caffeine rush. "But—"

I paused, head ducked as I wiped up the soda on the floor, mind whirling. *Help help help.*

I didn't want to hurt Owen's feelings by just saying no, but I couldn't say yes because technically I *would* have a date soon. If only Aaron had actually asked me, then I'd have a real excuse.

Then again, if I was totally positive Aaron was going to ask . . .

Straightening up, I tossed the paper towels in the trash can and forced myself to smile at Owen. "But the thing is, I've already got a—um—a date." Ugh, *why* did my voice have to sound so strange?

Owen was suddenly very busy getting the soda back out of the fridge. "Oh, okay!" he said, and his voice was all weird, too. "I didn't know, sorry."

"That's okay!"

The way he was focused on pouring more soda, you'd think he was performing brain surgery. I pressed a clammy hand to my cheek, willing my face to return to a normal shade. Worf's tongue lolled out as he looked back and forth between us, like this was the most entertainment he'd had in days.

When Mrs. Grady entered the kitchen, we both jumped. "So, Holly, you staying for pizza?" she asked cheerfully.

"Oh!" I realized I'd never called Dad to ask. "I'd love to, but . . . um . . . I just remembered my aunt's supposed to come over for dinner tonight, so I can't." *Never mind that she lives in Boston.*

"Ah, well, maybe next time." Mrs. Grady started rifling through a drawer, then pulled out a menu. Owen and I looked at anything but each other.

"I guess I should be going," I said to Worf.

"Okay, I'll walk you out," Owen said to the soda bottle.

We walked out of the kitchen and through the foyer in silence. Owen pulled the front door open all formally for some reason. I had a weird moment where I couldn't remember how we usually said good-bye. *Hug? Shake hands?* For a split second I lost my head entirely and started raising my hand to high-five him, then tucked my hair behind my ear instead.

I swallowed, hoping to get rid of that horrible cheerleader voice. "Well, see you tomorrow!" I squawked. Ugh.

"Sure, see you!"

Our eyes met just for a second, then he shut the door and I spun around and started walking. Fast.

Why why why why why why why. Why did Owen have to ask me to the dance? Not that I was mad that he did. Actually, I was kind of flattered, although right now that particular emotion was buried under a huge pile of horror at how awkward everything had become.

My head was buzzing. Did Owen like me? Like, *like* me like me? I picked up the pace, my feet matching the rapid pounding of my heart. I pictured how panicked Owen had looked. The way he had held his hands out, as if to say *stop!*

I meant just as friends. Just friends. If you want to. I thought it'd be fun.

I slowed down a little bit, replaying the whole thing from the beginning. Owen had asked me to go to the dance with him. Specifically, he said *Would you go to the dance with me?* Not *be my date* or anything like that. And

I had spit soda all over the kitchen. I groaned out loud, my face heating up all over again.

I was so busy wallowing in my own humiliation that when a car pulled up next to me and honked, I just about jumped out of my skin.

"Dad!"

He rolled down the window and gave me his Explain Yourself Young Lady look. Glancing around, I suddenly remembered where I was. I never walked home from Owen's, it was too far from my house. It also dawned on me that I was freezing.

"Where were you going?" Dad asked when I slid into the front seat. "You knew I was picking you up at six thirty. And where's your jacket?"

"I'm sorry, I just . . ." I shook my head, staring out the front window. "I was walking home. I forgot my jacket."

Dad glanced at me. "Okay, what's going on?"

"What? Nothing!" Stupid shrill voice.

"Did you have a fight with that boy—Owen?"

"What? No!" I exclaimed. "I just . . . I don't know what I was doing. I wasn't thinking. I'm sorry, I really am."

Dad waited a few seconds, then sighed and pulled away from the curb. "Well, it's a good thing I happened to pass you," he said, but he didn't lecture me anymore after that. For the moment. I was pretty sure he was saving it for later, though. And Mom was going to flip out when she found out I was just wandering around completely alone outside at night.

At home, I sprinted up the stairs, shut my bedroom door, grabbed my phone, and dialed Julia's number before Dad had even made it inside the house.

"Hello?"

"Julia, it's me. I was hanging out with Owen after school, and out of nowhere he asked me to the dance, and now everything is insanely weird, and I don't know what to do!"

I took a deep breath, waiting for her to say *Oh my God!* or *Are you serious?* or something like that.

"Aww!"

I pulled the phone away from my ear for a second and stared at it like it had grown fangs. "Did you just say *aww?*" I said in disbelief.

"Yes." I could hear the smile in her voice.

"*Aww* as in *awwkward?*"

"No," she said, laughing. "*Aww* as in aww, that's so cute!"

"Cute?!" I sputtered. "No, Julia, he—we—I just—"

"Holly, breathe," Julia ordered. Obediently, I inhaled, then exhaled. "Okay, now start from the beginning."

I did. I told her the whole thing, every single humiliating detail. When she finally spoke, I could tell she was trying not to laugh again.

"Do you think he likes you?"

"No," I said, and I meant it. "I really do think he meant just as friends. But then I freaked out and spit Coke all over the place, so now he probably thinks *I* think he likes me. We could barely even look at each other, Julia."

"Okay, so it's awkward right now," Julia said. "But it was just a misunderstanding, and you both know it. I'm sure things will go back to normal soon."

I wished I was as sure of that as she sounded. "I guess. I feel really bad about lying to him, though."

"You lied?"

"Well, sort of, yeah." Cradling the phone between my cheek and shoulder, I started reorganizing my dresser. "I mean, I told him I had a date, right? But I don't, not yet."

"True," Julia said slowly. "But that's kind of a technicality, though. I mean, you *know* Aaron's going to ask you, and he's the one you really want to go with."

"Right." I felt marginally better. "And saying I have a date is a whole lot less embarrassing than saying, 'Sorry, but I heard this other guy wants to ask me to the dance, and I'm going to say yes because I have a massive crush on him.'"

Julia giggled. "Does Owen know you like Aaron?"

"No!" I exclaimed, fumbling with a picture frame. "No, we don't talk about . . . stuff like that."

"Well, either way, it doesn't really matter," Julia said. "Aaron's going to ask you, you'll say yes, and I'm sure things will be okay with Owen."

"Right," I agreed, but deep down I wasn't so sure.

Chapter Seven

$\mathcal{T}$his is how things were supposed to go on Monday: I'd find Aaron at his locker before school and ask him to the dance. If he wasn't there, I'd ask him right before band.

Then I'd spend lunch discussing outfit possibilities for the dance with Julia and Natasha.

Then I'd get to science and joke with Owen about what a spaz I was on Friday so we could laugh about it and go back to normal.

The thought of asking Aaron out still made me feel like there were hummingbirds zipping around in my stomach, but I was tired of waiting for him to ask me. I had to get it over with. Even if there was a very real chance I'd lose my breakfast all over his shoes.

As it turned out, that didn't matter. Because nothing went according to plan.

I checked the band hall before school, then hung out with Julia in front of her locker (which was right next to Aaron's), but he never showed up. Then in PE, Coach Hoffman got mad when a few kids kept trying to hang from the hoop during basketball, so she made us all run an extra lap. Which meant I was still changing clothes when the bell rang. I had to sprint to the band hall and barely had time to grab my horn before Mr. Dante started rehearsal.

"Everything okay?" Gabby asked me as I slid past her and Natasha and slumped down in my chair.

"Stellar," I replied, still trying to catch my breath. I snuck a glance at Owen, but he kept his eyes fixed on his folder.

I wasn't the only one having an off day. Natasha, who was usually pretty much perfect during rehearsals, kept making the weirdest mistakes. Twice when Mr. Dante asked to hear just the brass, she spaced out and raised her horn up only after the rest of us had started playing. And she kept playing B-flats instead of B-naturals in "Festive Yuletide," even though Mr. Dante had given us the music a week ago.

"Is something wrong?" I whispered to her while he worked with the flutes.

"What?" Natasha's face went pink. "Oh no! Everything's great. I mean, not great. Fine, everything's fine."

Gabby and I shared a look. Something was clearly going on.

When Mr. Dante told us to pack up, I was hit with a fresh wave of nerves. No excuses this time—I'd just ask

Aaron now. In the cubbies, I put my horn away slowly, hoping the crowd would thin out enough so that the whole band didn't hear what I was about to do. Owen accidentally bumped my elbow with his case, mumbled a "sorry," and practically sprinted out of the band hall. *One awkward thing at a time,* I told myself. *You'll fix everything with Owen fifth period.*

Natasha seemed to be in kind of a hurry, too. Usually the three of us walked to lunch together, but she and Julia took off pretty quickly. *Julia probably filled her in on my plan,* I figured. They knew I'd be more nervous if they were there when I asked Aaron to the dance.

Taking in a deep, shaky breath, I turned to Aaron. Or rather, I turned to where Aaron had been standing a second ago. Stepping outside of the cubbies, I saw the doors swing closed behind him, Liam, and a few other guys.

Perfect.

Julia raised her eyebrows expectantly when I sat down at our table, but I just shook my head. Natasha didn't seem to notice our silent exchange. She was focused on trying to stab a straw into a juice box.

"Need some help?" Julia took the straw before Natasha could answer, stuck it in the box, then gave Natasha a pointed look. "Okay, what's going on with you?"

"What do you mean?" Natasha's voice was high and forced and oddly familiar. After a second, I realized why—she sounded just like I had with Owen.

"Did something happen?" I said. "You were kind of . . . off in band today. It's really unlike you."

"Yeah, I know." She giggled, which made the whole thing even weirder. Natasha took band as seriously as I did. "I guess I'm just nervous. All-region this weekend and all. How are you doing on the fugue?" she asked me.

I swallowed a bite of sandwich without chewing and coughed. All-region was Saturday. Great, just what my stomach needed. At this rate, I'd have to ask Dad for some of his ulcer medicine.

"Better," I said hoarsely. But the truth was I hadn't even played it since before the volleyball game. "You?"

"Yeah, better," she said, her voice still way too perky. "Those couple of measures near the end are still kind of hit or miss, but I think the rest of it sounds pretty good."

We spent the rest of lunch talking about all-region. Or rather, Natasha did. Anytime Julia or I tried to change the subject, she'd go off again about whether or not we'd have to play in front of other kids, what time she should get there, or what being in a band with kids from other schools would be like if she actually made it. A few minutes before lunch ended, Natasha suddenly jumped off the bench.

"I forgot my Spanish book in the band hall again!" she exclaimed, laughing that strange, high laugh. "I don't know what's wrong with me."

"That makes three of us," Julia said once she'd left the cafeteria. "What is up with her today?"

"I was hoping you'd know," I replied, shrugging. "She hasn't said anything to me."

"Nope, me neither." Julia glanced up when the bell rang. "I've got math with her right now. I'll find out what the deal is."

𝄞

When I got to science, I hesitated in the doorway. Owen was already at his desk, pencil flying over his sketchbook.

For a second, I debated on just acting like nothing had happened. But I knew better than that. The best thing to do would be to rip off the Band-Aid.

Squaring my shoulders, I headed to my desk.

"Hi, Owen!"

"Hi, Holly." He glanced up at me for the briefest of seconds.

"Hey, sorry about Friday."

That caught him off guard. He looked up at me, blinking furiously. "What?"

Sinking down into my chair, I tried to smile at him. "For, you know, freaking out. Spitting Coke all over the place." My voice was a little high, but at least it wasn't doing that cheerleader thing again. "I know you only asked me to the dance as friends."

His face relaxed just a tiny bit. "Oh. Don't worry about it."

I breathed a sigh of relief. "Thanks."

Owen glanced back at his sketchbook, then looked at me again. "Holly?"

"Yeah?"

"Are you, um . . . ?" He blinked. "Can I borrow your highlighter?"

"Sure." I dug it out of my backpack and handed it to him, and he smiled and said thanks. But I knew that wasn't what he really wanted to ask me, because I could see the green tip of his own highlighter sticking out of his overstuffed pencil bag.

Still, things were much less awkward already. After Mrs. Driscoll went over today's chapter, we headed to our lab stations. Owen and I joked around as usual while we examined different plant cells under the microscope. It wasn't completely normal, though. More like two people pretending things were normal. But I figured that couldn't last forever. At least, I hoped not.

$$\oint$$

I was already powering on my computer when Julia got to seventh period.

"Everything's okay with Owen," I told her, typing in my password. "I mean, it's still kind of weird, but I guess maybe things will just have to be weird for a while, and eventually they'll go back to normal. Don't you think?"

"Yeah, definitely." Julia pressed the power button on her computer, chewing the inside of her cheek. I glanced at her.

"Something wrong?"

After a few seconds, she tore her eyes away from her screen and looked at me. My stomach sank. Something was up, and whatever it was, I had the feeling I wasn't going to like it.

"I talked to Natasha," Julia said. "You know, about why she was acting so weird today."

"Is she okay?" I asked immediately.

"Yeah, it's just . . ." Julia squeezed her eyes shut briefly. "Ugh, Holly. I hate having to tell you this." Sighing, she turned her chair so that she was facing me.

"Aaron asked Natasha to the dance."

I didn't say anything.

"It was right before band, in the cubbies," Julia went on quickly. "Natasha said she was really surprised, she wasn't expecting him to or anything . . . and she, um . . . she said yes." She stopped, giving me a worried look. "Holly?"

The bell rang, and Ms. Vanzetti started giving instructions on our assignment for today. Which was a good thing, because I had no idea what to say to Julia. I just stared blankly at my screen.

Aaron liked Natasha.

My chest felt hollow, like there was a little hole in there growing bigger and bigger by the second.

I could feel Julia staring at me. When Ms. Vanzetti moved to the other side of the lab to help someone, Julia leaned closer. She didn't say anything, just waited. I blinked a few times, then shook my head.

"I don't get it," I said at last, my voice hoarse. "I didn't even know they . . ."

"I guess they talk a lot after school," Julia said. "And, you know, they ended up hanging out when their group met to bake all that stuff for the volleyball game last week." She paused. "Holly, Natasha is really, really worried about this. She's so afraid of hurting your feelings."

Julia's words barely registered. What was it Gabby had told me? I replayed it in my head, because it was a distraction from that horrible gnawing feeling that was getting worse by the second. Sophie had overheard Liam say something to Aaron about asking someone to the dance, and Aaron had said he'd been about to, but they were interrupted.

That was right after the volleyball game. And suddenly, I knew exactly what had happened. In my mind, I saw Aaron and Natasha on the other side of the gym, talking. I saw Trevor, arms flailing, falling straight back into our table and bringing the whole game to a halt. That was it—Aaron had been about to ask Natasha to the dance that night, but he was cut off because of Trevor's accident.

So this whole time it was Natasha he really liked.

Finally, I turned to look at Julia. "So she . . . she likes him, then?"

Julia was quiet for a second. "I think . . . I think that's something you should ask Natasha, not me."

After school, I walked to Natasha's house so slowly you'd think there were lead balls chained to my feet. Honestly, I wasn't sure what I was going to say, or even if I really wanted to talk to her yet. But I knew that if I put it off, things would be even weirder between us tomorrow. It was just like with Owen—I had to get it over with.

Two Band-Aid rippings in one day. No wonder I felt so raw.

I stood on the Prynnes' porch for a solid minute before finally ringing the bell. When Natasha opened the door and saw me, her eyes widened the same way they had when she saw the toothless zombie clowns at the Asylum.

"Holly!" She tried to smile, but it was shaky.

"Hey." I tried to smile back. "Um . . . can I come in?"

"Yeah! Sure!" That weird perky voice again. I was surprised to find I suddenly felt bad for Natasha. She'd probably been obsessing over talking to me about this all day. Just like I'd been so worried about fixing things with Owen.

When did keeping friendships get so hard? I wondered as I followed her into the kitchen.

"Want a drink?" Natasha asked, opening the fridge. "We've got lemonade, orange juice . . . I think there's some soda in here somewhere . . ."

I thought about Owen and the Coke and almost laughed. "Nah, I'm okay."

"Okay." She closed the door, and neither of us spoke for a few seconds.

This was how things used to be between me and Natasha—majorly uncomfortable. Except it's different now. We used to *want* to hurt each other's feelings, and now we're worried we will.

"Julia told me about Aaron," I said. *Rip.*

Natasha nodded, staring at her fingernails.

"I'm not mad or anything," I went on quickly. "I know you weren't . . . you know . . . *trying* to . . ."

"I wasn't, I promise!" Natasha's face was pink, and her eyes were suddenly watery. "I didn't know he was going to ask, it really surprised me, and I—I said yes, but Holly, I'll tell him I can't go if you want me to."

I gaped at her. "You would do that?"

Natasha nodded fervently. "I know you've liked him longer than—um, for a long time. I don't want this to mess up our friendship."

Despite how hurt I'd felt all day, I was touched. But at the same time, even though I knew it wasn't what Natasha intended, I felt even more humiliated. So she would tell Aaron she didn't want to go with him . . . and then what? I'd ask him, knowing he didn't like me that way?

Being second chair to Natasha in band was one thing—that's how band worked. But this was different. It wasn't just that I wanted to go to the dance with Aaron; I wanted *him* to want to go with *me*. But he didn't, so . . .

"You should go with him," I said. Natasha stared at me.

"What?"

"You like him, right?" *Please, please just admit it, I* thought.

She hesitated, then nodded.

"Yeah. I do."

I smiled at her. "Then you should go with him. It's totally fine," I added when she started to protest. "Really. We're still friends, I promise."

Natasha let out a shaky laugh, wiping her eyes. "You really are the best, Holly," she said, and we hugged. My own eyes were dry, but I could feel the tears building up.

I could hold them in until I got home, though. I was getting pretty good at that.

Chapter Eight

*T*uesday was stellar.

Julia found me practicing in the band hall before school (because there was no way I was going to hang out around Aaron's locker now). She came into my practice room just as I finished running through Fugue in F Minor for the tenth time.

"Sounds great!" she said brightly.

I shrugged. "It's getting better. I still mess up the last four measures every other time, though."

Julia waved a hand dismissively. "You're going to do awesome at all-region auditions on Saturday. I bet you make it."

Setting my horn down, I smiled at her. "I'm okay, Julia. You don't have to do this."

"Do what?"

"You know." I slid the music back into my folder. "Being extra nice because of the whole Aaron and Natasha thing. I'm fine, I promise. And I talked to

Natasha yesterday, by the way."

"Yeah, I know," Julia said. "She called me. But that's the first time we've ever talked about it," she added hurriedly. "Honestly, Holly, I had *no* idea she liked him and—"

"It's fine," I said, wondering if *fine* was going to become my word of the week. "I know."

Julia watched me reorganize my sheet music. "Holly . . ."

"Yeah?" I stood up, folder in one hand and horn in the other. Julia stood, too, and gave me a quick hug. And even though I appreciated it, I sort of wished she hadn't, because my throat got really tight.

"I'm really, really sorry," she said.

I swallowed. "I know. But don't worry, I'm okay. Really."

Maybe if I kept saying it, eventually it would be true.

When I got to English first period, there was a bag of M&M's on my desk.

"Thanks," I said to Gabby, who gave me a sympathetic smile.

"Anytime," she replied. "Look, Holly, I heard about Aaron and Natasha, and I'm so—"

"It's *fine*." It came out sharper than I intended, and Gabby held her hands up in defense.

"Okay. Sorry."

I felt kind of bad, but more than that, I was starting to get annoyed. It was humiliating enough that I'd spent the past few weeks so sure that Aaron liked me. All this pity made me feel even worse.

I was dreading band so much, I actually found myself wanting PE to last longer. How completely pathetic. But right now, eternal laps sounded way more appealing then sitting in the middle of the Triangle of Extreme Awkward.

Because that's what band had become. For fifty excruciating minutes, I tried to focus on rehearsal. But just two seats over to my left was the guy who'd asked me to the dance and who I'd turned down because I thought I was going with the guy seated directly behind me, who ended up asking the girl sitting on my right, who *knew* I had a crush on him and had secretly liked him the whole time, too.

It was kind of hard to concentrate on music.

But hey, at least I didn't have to deal with awkwardness at lunch. Not.

Back when Natasha and I hated each other, lunch consisted of us making catty remarks back and forth while Julia barely said a word. Now that we were trying so hard *not* to hurt each other's feelings, Julia couldn't stop talking.

"So then Kelly and I got up to recite our scene, but I think Ms. Jacobs missed, like, half of it because she kept trying to tell Mark to take off that wig. She seriously didn't believe him that it was actually stuck on until finally she went over and yanked on it and he screamed. It was so funny! I bet she totally regrets having us do these skits—Holly, you guys are studying Shakespeare in English, too, right? But I bet Mr. Franks doesn't make you get up and act out scenes from *Romeo and Juliet* in class. Oh hey, did I tell you guys what happened in PE yesterday?"

After three days, I couldn't take it anymore. I knew why Julia was talking so much—she was just trying to keep the subject away from Aaron. But if the three of us never just talked about it, it would only get more awkward. I mean, what if Natasha ended up being his girlfriend? We couldn't skirt the subject forever. No matter how much it made me feel like my heart had shriveled up like a raisin.

So when we sat down at our lunch table Thursday, I turned to Natasha before Julia could say a single word.

"Hey, have you found a dress for the dance yet?"

Natasha's mouth fell open, but she closed it quickly. I gave her an encouraging smile, unwrapping my sandwich. Julia was frozen with one hand in her lunch bag.

"Uh...no, not yet," Natasha replied at last. "Actually, I think my mom's taking me shopping Sunday. What about you?"

I shook my head. "I heard Milanie's is having a sale this weekend, though—you should check it out! They always have cute stuff."

Out of the corner of my eye, I saw Julia relax a tiny bit. Natasha smiled gratefully at me.

"Okay, I will. Thanks, Holly."

Things were a little better after that. Still, I was mentally drained by the time I got to science. Owen didn't seem to be in a very talkative mood, either, so we didn't chat much while we did our lab. I didn't think anything was wrong, though. Not until he said, "We can't hang out after school today."

I looked up from my worksheet, startled. Owen was busy cleaning the microscope slides and putting them back in their cases.

"Oh." I could feel myself starting to blush. "Um, okay. Why?"

"Megan's got a recital at school. I promised Mom I'd go. Sorry," he added, glancing at me.

"It's fine," I said lightly. "We'll catch up next week. *Cyborgs versus Ninjas*, right? I've got a bet to win."

"Right." Owen smiled, but it looked forced.

Owen wouldn't lie. He just wouldn't. That's what I told myself over and over during my last two agonizingly slow classes. If he said his stepsister had a recital, it must be true.

That didn't stop a nagging voice in my head from insisting that he just didn't want to hang out with me anymore, though. I thought apologizing on Monday would make things better with Owen, that eventually things would go back to normal. But if I was really honest with myself, things were slowly getting worse.

Maybe nothing would ever be normal again, with Owen *or* Natasha.

Chapter Nine

I stayed after school to practice my all-region piece some more. Partly because I was nervous about auditions, partly because when I told Mom before school that I wasn't going to Owen's, she kept asking why. I still didn't feel like talking about it.

I practiced before and after school on Friday, too. One good thing about all my friendships falling apart—I knew Fugue in F Minor backward and forward. The last few measures were still kind of rocky, but I was starting to think I might actually pull it off tomorrow.

Saturday morning, I stood by the front door with my horn case at my feet, checking my music folder for the hundredth time. "Mom, we're going to be late!" I hollered.

She poked her head out of the kitchen. "That letter you brought home from Mr. Dante said to be at the high school at nine."

"So?"

"It's seven thirty, Holly."

"But there might be traffic!"

Mom sighed. "Honey, the high school is less than a mile from here and it's Saturday morning. I think we'll be okay. Besides, you need to eat something."

My stomach squirmed at the thought. "No way. Too nervous."

"Just come in here, okay?"

Ugh. I left my folder on top of my horn case and trudged obediently into the kitchen. After last week's walking-home-from-Owen's incident, I wasn't in the mood for another lecture. (Even worse, Dad had told Mom he thought I was having "boy problems." Which, well, maybe it was true, but it was so not anything I wanted to talk about with my parents.)

Mom sat back down at the table, cradling a mug of coffee in her hands. The letter from Mr. Dante was next to her napkin.

"According to this, you won't know what time you audition until the schedule is up in the cafeteria at nine," Mom said. "For all you know, you won't play until noon. You really need to eat something."

"Mom, do you *want* to see me throw up?"

She rolled her eyes. "Just something small. Grab a cereal bar."

Dutifully, I crossed the kitchen, opened the pantry door, and grabbed the box of cereal bars. "Empty," I said, showing Mom. "You'd think Chad could take two seconds and throw the box away."

Mom snorted. "It's worse with the pickles. I swore for weeks the pickles tasted like Doritos, then sure enough, one day I caught him fishing around the jar right after eating a whole bag of chips. All the cheese powder was floating around in the pickle juice."

I stared at her in horror. "*What?*"

"Never mind," Mom said quickly, adding sugar to her mug.

I was so never putting pickles on my sandwich again.

"Anyway, you need to eat." Mom glanced around. "Maybe a banana?"

I pointed to the empty fruit bowl, and she sighed again.

"Right. I'm going to the grocery this afternoon." She took a sip of coffee. "We have cornflakes, I know that much. And there are a few eggs left—want me to scramble them up?"

My response was a gagging noise.

"Holly. You are not leaving this house until you've eaten a bite of something."

I groaned loudly. "Fine." Glancing around the kitchen, my gaze landed on the gleam of plastic wrappers over by the phone. I grabbed one and slumped back down in my chair.

"A fortune cookie," Mom said wryly. "Breakfast of champions."

I broke the cookie open and popped half into my mouth, making a face at her. Then I glanced at the slip of paper.

FAIL TO PREPARE AND PREPARE TO FAIL

Awesome.

By the time we got to the high school (which, admittedly, only took five minutes), I was even more queasy. It turned into full-blown nausea when I looked out of the car window and saw dozens of unfamiliar kids carrying instrument cases and drumstick bags.

"Good luck, honey!" Mom said, and I smiled and tried not to look like I wanted to vomit.

"Thanks!"

Clutching my case and my folder, I pushed through the front entrance with my shoulder and stared around. There was the main office, all dark and locked up at the far end of the giant foyer. Everyone seemed to be heading down the hall on the right, where I noticed a giant sign that said ALL-REGION taped to the wall, with an arrow beneath it. I headed that way, too, suddenly feeling very small. Why were the ceilings in this place so insanely high? Like high schoolers were all twenty feet tall or something.

Every classroom door had a sign taped to it, too, with things like CLARINET—4 and BARITONE—2 written on them. By the time I reached the cafeteria, I was seriously wishing I hadn't eaten that cookie.

It looked like at least a hundred kids were here already. Some were at the tables, opening their cases—a few were already starting to warm up. There was a crowd in front of the wall next to the vending machines, where I saw several sheets of paper taped in a long line. I pushed my way through and squinted until I found *French horn*.

Whoa. There were a *lot* of horn players here. I scanned down the list and found my name.

Holly Mead (Millican)—Group 8—Room 3—10:52 a.m.

"Where's room three?" I spoke out loud without really meaning to. A girl with a blond braid and braces next to me pointed to the paper taped at the very end.

"That one's a map. All the rooms are labeled."

"Thanks!" I edged through the crowd until I stood in front of the map. French horn—room three turned out to be in D-hall on the second floor. In fact, all of the brass rooms were in second-floor classrooms, and all of the woodwinds were on the first floor. The percussionists were in the band hall and the choir room.

Turning, I moved away from the schedule and stared around the cafeteria, wondering if Julia was here yet. No sign of her—or Gabby or Natasha, for that matter.

I headed upstairs and found the classroom with the FRENCH HORN—3 sign. Two boys from another school were already there, sitting up against the wall. The room's schedule was posted next to the door. I scanned it quickly. Brooke was in group five at 9:32, but Natasha and Owen were apparently in one of the other rooms. I didn't recognize any of the other names in my group.

Mr. Dante had told us that the judges weren't allowed to see us, or even know our names. He said they would be sitting behind a curtain, and that we weren't supposed to talk when we were in the room—the room monitor would just give the judges our number. That way they wouldn't know who was from which school. It helped me to calm down a little when I reminded myself that at least the judges wouldn't be sitting there staring at me.

But four other French horn players would.

Glancing up at the clock, I sighed and headed back down to the cafeteria. It was even more crowded now, and I spotted a few familiar faces. Leah Collins was sitting against the wall with her music spread on the floor, drumming on the bottom of her shoe. Not far from her, Liam was asleep with his head on his tuba case.

I set my horn case and music folder down at an empty table on the far end of the cafeteria. It was too early to start warming up now, so instead I just stared at Fugue in F Minor and willed my stomach to stop jumping. But it felt like I'd eaten the paper along with the fortune cookie and now the words were poking and jabbing inside my stomach.

Prepare.

To.

Fail.

Around me, more and more kids were taking out their instruments and warming up. After half an hour of trying to keep my cookie down, I pulled out my horn and slowly played through a few scales before trying the fugue.

But the last few measures I'd worked on so hard were just not happening this morning. After a few minutes, I gave up and put my horn back in its case. Might as well go upstairs and get this over with.

"Holly!"

Natasha was making her way to my end of the table. I cringed, hoping she hadn't heard me flub the end of the fugue that last time.

"Hi!"

"I just wanted to say good luck before I leave," she said. "I checked the schedule to see when you were going. Poor Julia's not until after two. She just went home—her dad's bringing her back later. We were looking for you earlier!"

"Yeah, it's pretty crowded," I said, glancing around. "So you played already? How'd it go?"

Natasha wrinkled her nose. "Not bad, I guess. The scales were fine. It definitely wasn't the best I've ever played the fugue, though."

Yeah right, I couldn't help but think. "I'm sure you did great."

After we said good-bye, I trudged up the stairs. Several dozen trumpet and horn players were sitting along both sides of the hallway now, some fingering through their music, but most just chatting. I slid down to the floor right across from my room and took out my horn.

It wasn't like Natasha to be self-deprecating, even just a little bit. Maybe she just said that to me out of pity. She probably sounded amazing, as always. I figured she'd at least make the concert band—that was the second all-region band. Then I rolled my eyes. Who was I kidding? This was Natasha. She'd probably make the symphonic band.

I frowned, pressing my valves extra hard as I fingered through the last few measures of the fugue. The pity thing was getting old. I almost wished Natasha would go back to being stuck-up and arrogant like she was when we first met. That would be easier to deal with than this whole "let's be extra sensitive to poor Holly" routine.

Closing my eyes, I leaned my head back and tried to take deep, long breaths. I had to focus on this audition. On my third inhalation, I smelled a familiar piney-grapefruit smell and opened my eyes just as Aaron passed me. He stopped four doors down, checked the schedule next to the sign, then sat down against the wall.

Sadness settled like a rock in the pit of my stomach. He hadn't even noticed me. But then again, why would he? It wasn't like he liked me or anything.

I was so busy wallowing in my own misery, I barely noticed when a red-haired girl with a horn sat down across the hall from me, and then a boy. When the door to room three opened a few minutes later, I jumped, then shrank back as a group of kids filed out.

The room monitor, a tired-looking guy Chad's age in a Ridgewood High School Band shirt, held the door open with his foot and consulted his clipboard.

"Group eight?"

Focus, I tried to tell myself, getting shakily to my feet. But I couldn't stop thinking about Aaron. Aaron and Natasha. Natasha and Aaron. I wondered if she'd found him this morning to say good luck, too.

Five chairs and five music stands were arranged in a semicircle in the middle of the room. At the front was a long, tall black curtain. I heard someone cough on the other side.

I sat down in the chair on the far left, not looking at the other kids. A piece of paper was taped to each music stand.

#5—Scales

B♭ (Concert E♭)

A♭ (Concert D♭)

E♭ (Concert A♭)

"Number one goes first, then two, and so on. Play the scales first, in the order they appear on your sheet," the room monitor instructed us. "Then the étude, Fugue in F Minor. If you need something, raise your hand and I'll come over—don't talk to the judges, okay?"

We nodded.

"Okay. Number one, you're up."

He stepped back. The red-haired girl, who was sitting in the chair on the far right, cast a nervous glance at the rest of us and lifted her horn to her lips.

Number five—I was last. *Stellar.*

The red-haired girl started out pretty shaky on the scales, but sounded stronger on the étude. Still, I knew I could play it better. Alone, in my practice room, when my fingers weren't trembling with nerves.

"Number two, go ahead."

The next boy started playing the étude first, and the room monitor had to stop him and remind him to play the scales. I winced. How embarrassing.

I realized I was tapping furiously on my knee, and clenched my hand in a fist. *Relax,* I told myself. *Think about something else.*

But that didn't help, because of course the first thing I thought of was Aaron walking right past me. Aaron dancing with Natasha. Aaron, Aaron, Aaron . . .

"Number five?"

Startled, I glanced up to see the room monitor looking at me expectantly. Instinctively, I opened my mouth to respond, but caught myself just in time.

Raising my horn to my lips, I took a deep breath and played through the three scales. I could hear the scribbling of pencils on the other side of the curtain as I adjusted my music stand and stared at Fugue in F Minor. Lifting my horn, I began to play.

But I wasn't really seeing the notes or thinking about tone or counting rhythms. It was ridiculous, but I still just couldn't stop thinking about Aaron not even noticing me in the hall. And Natasha, feeling so sorry for me. Gabby buying me M&M's, Owen bailing on *Prophets* day, Julia nervously rambling on and on . . .

And then, before I knew it, it was over. Blinking in confusion, I set my horn in my lap.

"Don't forget your folders," the room monitor was saying. "And please don't talk on your way out."

I followed the other four kids out of the room, heart beating so loud i barely heard the monitor call for group nine.

"Hey, Holly!" Victoria waved to me at the end of the hallway. "Did you play already? How did it go?"

"Um . . . fine!" I replied. "Good, I think."

Which was a total lie. Because somehow I had played the entire fugue and not heard a note.

Chapter Ten

When I talked to Julia on the phone Saturday night, I told her the same thing I told Victoria.

"Fine! I did fine. I think."

"I'm sure you did better than fine," Julia said. "I mean, geez. You practiced before *and* after school practically every day this week. You could probably play that music in your sleep."

Which was true. But I still wasn't nearly as confident in myself as she seemed to be.

It poured rain on Sunday. Since Julia was visiting her aunt, I spent the whole day watching movies and reading. Or really, pretending to watch movies and read. In reality, I was just going over and over my audition in my head. I remembered sitting in the chair and looking at the scale sheet, and the room monitor telling me to start. I remembered finishing and leaving the room.

But the fugue was still just a blur.

I mean, I remembered *some* details, like little

fragments. And I was fairly certain I hadn't stopped or stumbled at any point, or made any constipated moose sounds (as my brother so often said I did). I didn't do *badly*.

That didn't mean I'd done great, though. Or even good.

By Monday morning, the rain hadn't let up. When I walked into the band hall to put my horn up, I heard Aaron's voice, turned abruptly, and went back into the hall. Then I waited out of sight until the bell rang and he left before shoving my case in its cubby and getting to English half a minute late.

I was officially pathetic.

Anyway, trying to avoid Aaron was pointless. Because when fourth period came, I still had to face the Triangle of Extreme Awkward. And today it would be even more awkward thanks to the all-region results, which Mr. Dante had posted on the window of his office.

Hovering in the band-hall entrance, I watched as more and more kids crowded around the results. I took my time getting my horn out, feeling sick. I knew there was no way I actually *made* either of the bands—not when I was competing against all those eighth-graders from other schools, and I couldn't even get first chair in my own school's band. But what if my performance had actually been horrible? What if I came in *last*? Out of every horn player in the district?

My legs felt like rubber as I slowly crossed the room. Trying to avoid eye contact with anyone, I slipped between Liam and Leah and found the concert band list.

French Horn

1. Adrian Walters (Jacksonville)
2. Jin Sheng-Yen (Hudson Park)
3. Natasha Prynne (Millican)
4. Kieran Holland (Forest Hill)

My eyes started to burn. I couldn't even bring myself to look at the rest of the list to see how far down I was. Taking a step back, I heard someone yelp and mumbled an apology. Blindly, I tried to make my way through the growing crowd around the results. I'd almost made it when someone grabbed my arm.

"Holly!"

I faced Gabby, blinking rapidly. She was beaming, shaking my arm and jumping up and down.

"What?" I said dumbly.

"What do you mean, *what?*" she yelled, laughing. "Symphonic band! Both of us!"

She had to be joking. Even though that would be a seriously evil joke. But I turned back to the window to look. My legs went all shaky again when I found the symphonic band list.

French Horn

1. Tanya Riding (Forest Hill)
2. Thomas Plank (Bryant)
3. Nikhil Bansal (Forest Hill)
4. Holly Mead (Millican)

I'd made it. I'd made the all-region band. The *first* one.

I just stood there, mouth hanging open, while Gabby bounced around me. A few hands patted me on the back, and a couple of kids said, "Congratulations, Holly!" But I couldn't move for anything.

Was it a fluke? I couldn't help but wonder. I mean, I'd never beaten Natasha on a chair test . . . and suddenly I wasn't just a few chairs ahead of her in all-region, I *was in the more advanced band.*

"Okay, folks. Bell rang two minutes ago."

At the sound of Mr. Dante's voice, everyone headed to their seats. My legs finally started to cooperate, and I trailed behind Gabby to my chair. When I got there, Natasha was sitting in it. I stopped, waiting for her to stand.

"Nope—you sit here now," she said with a grin, patting the chair to her right. "All-region audition results counted as a chair test, that's what Mr. Dante said. Remember?"

Whoa. I was first chair.

I sat down between Natasha and Gabby, still sort of in shock. Julia caught my eye and mouthed *Oh my God!*, beaming. Owen was taking his seat—three seats away from me now, instead of two. He'd probably be happy about that.

Gabby leaned really close and whispered in my ear. "Dude, we're the only seventh-graders from Millican who made the symphonic band!"

I let out a weird, shaky laugh. This was so not sinking in.

Suddenly, I remembered Natasha. Just what our friendship needed—more awkwardness.

"Thanks for practicing with me so much," I said quietly to her, just as Mr. Dante stepped up on the podium. "I guess it paid off for both of us!"

"Totally," she agreed, smiling. Was it my imagination, or did the smile not quite reach her eyes? "And, hey, congrats. Seriously. I'm really happy for you."

"Thanks," I said. And it looked like she meant it, too. But there was something else, something about the way she looked at me that took a minute to figure out. Natasha was . . . surprised. Surprised that I'd finally beaten her at something.

Well, I was surprised, too. And proud.

"So as you've all seen, Millican did phenomenally at all-region on Saturday," Mr. Dante said. "I've heard all of you working hard on that music over the last month, and I'm proud of everyone who auditioned. And, hey— we had a total of nineteen students in this room make one of the all-region bands!"

Wow. I suddenly realized I hadn't even looked to see who else had made it, other than Natasha and Gabby. Instinctively, I looked at Julia. When she noticed me, I made a little pointing motion at her. *Did you make it?* Grinning, she nodded and held up two fingers. *Second band.*

"For those of you in one of the two bands, I'll

have packets of information for you to take home over winter break," Mr. Dante went on. "The concert will be Saturday, February fifteenth, so you'll have two full days of rehearsals, starting Friday morning. You'll be excused from school, of course."

"That's it," I heard Trevor mutter behind me. "I'm practicing more next year."

After that, Mr. Dante talked a little bit about the fund-raiser and the next volleyball game. Then we started our warm-ups. I tried to pay attention, but I couldn't. It was slowly starting to sink in. All-region. Symphonic band. First chair. I felt like a helium balloon slowly inflating, ready to bob around the band-hall ceiling. By the time we finished our scales, it was hard to keep my embouchure set because my lips kept stretching into a huge smile against my will.

"Let's get out 'Labyrinthine Dances,'" Mr. Dante announced, flipping on the metronome. Several kids groaned.

Boop . . . boop . . . . boop . . .

"Come on, now," Mr. Dante said. "We've made a lot of progress! This is over twenty beats faster than the first time we rehearsed this piece."

"Labyrinthine Dances" was a ridiculously, insanely, impossibly hard song that Mr. Dante had given us at the beginning of the year. He had this crazy theory that if we rehearsed it really slow and gradually sped up, we'd be able to play it up to tempo in time for the big state contest at the end of the year.

The problem was that the tempo he started us at was so slow, we always felt like it would take us a whole year just to get all the way through it.

Not today, though. At least, not for me. By the time we were halfway through the first page, I could see a few flute players grimacing in frustration. Next to me, Gabby dramatically gasped for breath after holding out a particularly long note.

But I could have played "Labyrinthine Dances" all day. Right then, I felt like I could play *anything*.

𝄞

After rehearsal, I pretended to reorganize the music in my folders while everyone headed to the cubbies. I was itching to go find out who else had made the all-region bands, but I didn't want to be too obvious about it.

"Hey, Holly?"

I glanced up—Owen was standing just to my left. "Oh! Hey," I said, surprised.

"I just wanted to say congratulations," he said with a little smile. "You know, on the all-region thing. You deserve it."

I smiled back. "Thanks, Owen!" He walked off toward the cubbies, and I sat there for a second, feeling deflated. Why did things have to get so weird with Owen? I really missed him. The not-awkward him, I mean.

Standing slowly, I tucked my folder under my arm,

grabbed my horn, and headed back to the lists taped up in the office window.

Under each section in the concert band, there were two alternates, followed by a list of everyone else who played that instrument in the order the judges had ranked them. Julia was there, second-to-last chair in the concert band. In fact, there were a lot of "Millicans" in both the symphonic- and concert-band clarinet sections. No surprise there—our clarinet section was almost all eighth-graders, and really good.

There was Gabby, third alto sax. Aaron was in the symphonic band, too—whoa, second-chair trumpet. And Liam, third-chair tuba. Sophie Wheeler was an alternate on oboe, which was impressive considering there was only one oboe in each band and over a dozen had auditioned. Victoria and Leah were both in the concert band, too. Brooke was just a few chairs below the French horn alternate, and Owen was around the middle of the list.

I was almost finished counting the nineteen Millican names in the two bands when Mr. Dante's voice startled me.

"Great job, Holly. You must be pretty excited."

I couldn't help but grin. "Yeah. But kind of surprised, too."

He tilted his head. "Why?"

"Well, I mean . . ." I glanced over my shoulder. "I don't know. I thought if I made it I'd be in the concert band. I'm not . . . I'm not sure how I beat Natasha. I've never even beaten her in a chair test."

Glancing at the clock, Mr. Dante reached for the shelf over his desk and pulled out what I recognized as a few of our beginner-band books from last year— tuba, baritone, trombone. Fifth period was beginner low brass, I figured.

"Holly, you're always prepared for every chair test," he said, stacking the books on his desk. "But with the all-region music . . . I heard you last week. Back in the practice rooms before and after school, every day. All I can say is, I'm not at all surprised by the results."

I smiled, although my face was probably magenta. But part of me had sort of expected him to say, *Yeah, I have no idea how you beat Natasha, either.*

"Thanks," I said. "Although . . . something weird did kind of happen when I auditioned."

"What do you mean?" Mr. Dante asked.

All of a sudden, I had to tell him.

"I—I don't *remember* playing the fugue," I admitted. "I remember playing the scales, and then . . . I don't know. It's like I wasn't paying attention to myself or something. When I left the room, I really had no idea how I sounded."

As soon as it was out of my mouth, I wanted to take it back. I felt like a complete fraud.

But Mr. Dante smiled. "So you were in the zone."

"Huh?"

The bell rang, and all the background chatter started fading as everyone filed out of the band hall.

Mr. Dante picked up the beginner books.

"The zone," he repeated. "Your brain knew all the technical stuff—like we talked about last month, remember? The rhythms, the right notes, dynamics, all of that. You didn't have to think about it anymore. So let me ask you—if you weren't thinking about the music, what *were* you thinking about when you auditioned?"

I glanced over just in time to see the back of Aaron's head disappear when the doors swung closed. Natasha and Julia were waiting for me just outside the cubbies.

"Just . . . stuff," I mumbled, my face hot again.

Mr. Dante sounded like he was trying not to laugh. "Well, it sounds to me like you forgot about being 'perfect' and let your emotions kick in. You made music out of the fugue." Walking to the podium, he set the beginner books down and smiled at me. "Maybe you should start trying to get in the zone more often."

Chapter Eleven

The week before Thanksgiving was weird. I'd be happy one second and bummed the next, like someone was messing with a switch that controlled my emotions.

First of all, sitting first chair rocked. Winning isn't everything, second best is okay—yeah, I knew all that.

Still. It rocked.

And it seemed like maybe things really were getting better with Owen, too. In science class the day before break started, he even brought up our *Cyborgs versus Ninjas* bet.

"I think we should raise the stakes," he said, poking the dead worm on the tray in between us with a scalpel. "The winner should actually win something. Like with the fund-raiser."

"You want to wear a vampire Santa costume to the concert, too?" I asked, and he laughed.

"Fine, not *exactly* like the fund-raiser."

"Okay." I tapped my chin, pretending to think. "Let's see, what would I like to win . . ."

Shaking his head, Owen grinned. "You're so positive you're going to get it. There's no way, Holly."

I ignored this. "How about . . . your phantom blade."

His eyes widened, and for a second I felt a twinge of anxiety. The phantom blade was one of the best weapons in *Prophets*, and really hard to find. Owen had scored one in level six the last time we'd played—the day he'd asked me to the dance and I'd spewed soda and screwed everything up. Me asking if he'd bet the blade implied we were going to start having *Prophets* day again, and I still wasn't sure if that was something he wanted.

"All right," Owen said at last, and I relaxed a little. "But if *I* win . . . we swap tanks."

I gasped in mock horror. Every alien hunter in *Prophets* got to build their own tank, and mine was way better than Owen's. It was pretty much the only reason I was as good as I was at the game.

"If you're really so positive you'll win, you wouldn't be worried," Owen teased. I crossed my arms.

"Fine. If I win, I get the phantom blade. If you win—yeah, right—we swap tanks."

"Deal."

"Cool." I paused, staring at the worm. "So . . . want to watch it over Thanksgiving break?" He didn't answer right away, and my stomach squirmed. "I mean, we still need to work on those programs, too—the concert's in, like, three weeks."

"Oh, right." Owen fumbled with his scalpel. "The thing is, my grandparents are staying with us over the break, and my uncle, and . . ."

"It's okay," I said quickly, wishing I hadn't asked. "Maybe another time."

"Or you could watch it," he added. "Just the first half, I mean."

But I want to watch it with you. That's what I wanted to say. But I couldn't.

"How do you know I won't cheat?" I joked half-heartedly, and Owen rolled his eyes.

"Yeah, right."

I smiled, tapping my pencil on the worm diagram I was supposed to be labeling. "Okay, I'll watch the first half over the break."

Owen grinned. "Cool."

I left science class feeling pretty good.

But right after school, I had to run to Mr. Franks's room because I'd left my winter-break reading list on my desk. And that's when I saw Natasha and Aaron, laughing and walking so close their arms kept grazing. I watched as they went out the side exit to the buses. Just like that, someone flipped the switch and all my happiness vanished.

I was tired of feeling bad about Aaron liking Natasha. I wanted to be happy for her and just get over it. And really, I had no choice if we were going to stay friends.

Still—ow. Ow ow ow ow *ow.*

"Chad?" I knocked on my brother's door and waited. No answer. Pushing the door open, I stepped over the pile of laundry—which I swear was the same exact pile from a few weeks ago—and headed to the movie shelf.

"Cyborgs, cyborgs . . ." After a minute of searching, I found *Cyborgs versus Ninjas* stuck in the right corner of the third shelf. I took it, shaking my head. It had been way over a month ago that Chad's friend Leon had brought this over, but somehow I wasn't surprised it was still here.

Then I realized a bunch of Chad's—and my— movies were probably collecting dust over at Leon's and Toby's houses.

"That's it," I said out loud. Marching back to my room, I grabbed a pad of yellow paper, sticky notes, and a pencil.

An hour later, Chad walked into his room and froze, one dirty sneaker stepping on the mountain of clothes. "What are you doing?"

"Organizing," I replied without looking up. Stacks of DVDs surrounded my feet, each with a sticky note labeling it with things like *House—Invisible* and *Murder— Nightfall*.

"You can't just come into my room and—"

"Chad, give me a break," I interrupted. "You barge into my room whenever you want and you know it. Besides, look at *this*." Picking up the *Cyborgs* DVD, I held it out for him to see.

Chad squinted. "Oh yeah, that's Leon's. I meant to give that back."

"But you haven't," I said. "Because you didn't even know it was here. So how many of *our* DVDs does Leon have?"

"Uh—"

"Six!" I yelled, waving my yellow pad. "That I know of, anyway. Probably more. Geez, Chad—a lot of these are mine, you know. From birthdays and Christmas and allowance money. So I'm organizing them, and you're just going to have to deal with it."

Chad rubbed his forehead like he was getting a headache. "Okay, fine, whatever."

I stared as he stepped off the pile of laundry and started picking through shirts and sniffing them. Holding up a dark blue T-shirt, he inspected a stain on the sleeve. Then he pulled off his San Antonio Spurs jersey, tossed it on top of the pile, and pulled on the stained blue shirt.

"Are you kidding me?"

He glanced at me in surprise. "What?"

"Chad, you just traded a dirty shirt for another dirty shirt."

"*Less* dirty," he corrected me, heading to his computer.

"You do know we have these magical machines downstairs that, like, wash *and* dry clothes, don't you?"

Chad typed in his password, his back to me. "Yeah, but Mom said she and Dad won't do my laundry anymore."

I walked over to his desk. "They haven't done my laundry since I started middle school."

"Well, you're the freak fifth-grader who actually *wanted* to learn how to do it. I don't."

"So?" I said, kicking his chair. "Ever stop to think that it's kind of pathetic that a sixteen-year-old doesn't even know how to work a washing machine? Do you think Mom's going to come do your laundry when you go to college?"

"God, Holly," Chad groaned. "You sound *exactly* like her."

"I'll teach you," I offered. "It's easy, I swear."

"No, thanks."

"So what are you going to do, just wear the same dirty clothes forever?"

"Don't be stupid," Chad replied. "Christmas is next month. New clothes."

"Chad!" I cried. "You can't—you . . ." He snickered, starting up a computer game. My eyes fell on a few fortune cookies on his desk.

"You have to do your laundry," I said triumphantly, "because you have to clean your work uniform. Or were you just planning on asking your boss for a new Lotus Garden shirt every month?"

Chad's smirk faded. "Yeah, Mr. G. kind of said something about that last week." He tapped his fingers on the mouse, then looked at me. "You can do it."

"Never."

"I'll pay you."

"No." I paused. "How much?"

He considered it. "Fifty cents a load," he said. "What? What are you laughing at?"

"You're insane." I went back to organizing the shelf, and he went back to crashing race cars on his computer. Fifteen minutes later, the DVDs were neatly organized. I took a moment to admire my work before walking up behind Chad and tapping the back of his head with my yellow pad. He paused his game and glared at me.

"What?"

"Our movies are alphabetized on the shelf," I said, ripping off a sheet of paper and handing it to him. "Here's a list of the ones that are missing. When you get them back from Leon or Toby or whoever, I'll shelve them in the right place. Whenever you watch something, just put it back where you found it. I'm going to make a cross-referenced spreadsheet to keep track of everything and add new DVDs as we get them—I'll e-mail it to you."

He stared at me. "Right. I'm pretty sure *you're* the one who's insane."

I ignored him. "I'm borrowing this tonight," I went on, holding up *Cyborgs*. "You can bring it back to Leon on Monday."

"You know that's sci-fi, right?" Chad asked. "Not really your thing."

"I know," I said, shrugging. "But I promised someone I'd watch it."

"Ah," Chad said, grinning. "Your boyfriend. Who,

by the way, still has all those *Watch the Fog* movies. So I don't know what you're giving me such a hard time about."

"I know," I replied, trying to keep my voice normal. "I'll . . . I'll get them back next week. And it's not . . . um, that's a different guy."

"Wow, *two* boyfriends." Chad was enjoying himself, clearly oblivious to the fact that I wanted to crawl into a hole. "Have you told Mom and Dad about this?"

"There's nothing to tell," I said flatly. "They're both just friends." Before he could say anything else, I grabbed my yellow pad, sticky notes, and *Cyborgs,* and headed for the hall.

"By the way," I added, "ten bucks a load. That's my offer."

"*Ten?*" Chad cried. "No way!"

"Hey, you've got a job," I said. "I mean, until your boss fires you because some customer complains that his delivery boy smells rank."

"Come on, Holly—"

"Ten bucks a load, or you let me teach you how to do it yourself." I smiled sweetly. "For the one-time price of twenty dollars. Your choice." And with that, I closed the door.

Back in my room, I took the *Cyborgs* disc out of its case and slid it into my DVD player. I flopped down on my bed and hit PLAY. But when the opening credits started, I couldn't focus.

Aaron still had the first two *Watch the Fog* movies.

And *Carrie,* too. Even though I was alone in my room, a blush crept over my cheeks as I remembered my big, stupid plan to get Aaron to ask me to the dance. And then I realized how close I'd come to just asking him myself in the cubbies—the exact same day he'd asked Natasha. Well, at least I'd avoided *that* level of humiliation.

But I kept picturing it, anyway. How it would have happened. Me mustering up all my courage. *"Aaron, I was wondering if you'd go to the dance with me."*

Him looking all surprised. *"Uh, I've already got a date, Holly. With Natasha. What, did you actually think I liked you or something?"*

Not that Aaron would ever say anything like that. He was too nice. Still, my brain wouldn't let it go—I watched it happen over and over, like a scene on replay. When my phone rang, it was a relief to hit the mental pause button.

"Hello?"

"Hey, it's me," Julia said.

"Hey! Aren't you at your uncle's place?"

"Yes, and I'm losing my *mind,*" she moaned. "My cousins are driving me nuts. How about you?"

"I'm bored," I said, flipping my TV off. "I finally organized my and Chad's movies, though."

Julia laughed. "But that's your idea of fun!"

I smiled a little. "True. So . . . have you talked to Natasha?"

"Nope," she replied. "I was going to call her later. You?"

"Nah," I said, chewing my lip. "I, um . . . I saw her and Aaron leaving school together Wednesday."

"Yeah." I could hear the sympathy in Julia's voice. "I told you, they've got class right next to each other seventh, remember?"

"Yeah." I hesitated. "Do you know if . . . are they . . . you know, dating?"

"I don't think so," Julia said. "I mean, Natasha hasn't said anything other than they're going to the dance. I don't think they've hung out outside of school. Well, except for baking all that stuff for the fund-raiser—but that was with a bunch of people."

"Oh."

"Holly, are you okay? *Really* okay?"

"Yeah." I rolled my eyes—that sounded unconvincing, even to me. "No, I'm not. I'm not mad at her or anything," I added quickly. "I just feel so dumb. I can't believe I thought he liked me. And I just . . . *ugh*. I don't even think I want to go to the dance anymore."

"I'm really sorry." Julia sighed. "If it helps, I know Natasha feels really weird about it, too. She would have told him no if you wanted."

"I know," I said, ignoring a small flash of irritation. "But come on, how pathetic would that be? They like each other, they should go to the dance together. It doesn't really matter how I feel."

"It matters to Natasha," Julia said softly.

"Yeah," I mumbled. "I know."

"If you don't go to the dance, I'd totally understand,"

she continued. "But I really hope you do. I think it'd make you feel even worse if you *weren't* there. I missed the band party, remember? It was so depressing, being at home, thinking about all of you guys out having fun. And you *know* the dance is going to be awesome, right?"

She had a point. "Right," I said.

"So you're still going?"

I laughed. "Yeah. I'm going. And *you're* still asking Seth," I added. "I'm holding you to our pact."

Julia groaned, but I could tell she was smiling. "Okay, okay," she said. "And hey, I got a dress this morning! I can't *wait* for you to see it!" She started describing her dress in detail, and her shoes, and her new earrings. Her enthusiasm was pretty contagious, and by the time we hung up, I was grinning.

Maybe the dance *would* be fun. Maybe I'd get a new dress, too. Maybe it wouldn't be so bad to see Aaron and Natasha together. Dancing. Holding hands, even.

Well, I could at least *pretend* it wasn't so bad.

Sighing, I flipped my TV back on and watched about a minute of *Cyborgs* before turning it off again. I was supposed to watch this *with* Owen, and thinking about that just bummed me out even more. After a few minutes of feeling sorry for myself, I got up to go see if I could talk Chad into fifteen bucks for a lesson.

Laundry night with my brother. What a great Thanksgiving break this was turning out to be.

Chapter Twelve

*H*ow great would it be if someone invented a "get over it" button? You just press it and that's it—whatever's bothering you, whatever you're worried about, whatever guy with beautiful brown eyes and a smile you can't stop thinking about no matter how hard you try . . . gone. You're over it.

I got to school Monday morning determined to press that button, real or not. My crush on Aaron couldn't last now that I knew he liked someone else, right? There wasn't any point. And it wasn't like he was the only cute, nice guy out there. I knew tons of them. (Okay, maybe not *tons*. But some.)

So before the first bell, I went to Julia's locker as usual. And there he was, cramming books into his bag, loose papers falling to the floor. He glanced up and smiled at me.

"Hey, Holly! Have a good break?"

"Yup! Did you?" I asked, hating the butterflies

flapping around in my stomach. *He likes Natasha,* I told them, willing them to fly away. They didn't.

"Pretty good. Oh, thanks," he added when I caught a folder sliding out of his locker. His fingers grazed mine when I handed it to him, and my face got warm.

Yeah, there was no such thing as a "get over it" button.

"See you in band," Aaron said, and I said, "See you." It wasn't until he'd gone around the corner that I remembered the DVDs. He'd probably forgotten about them. Maybe they were lost forever in the pits of his messy locker.

I had the sudden, horrifying realization that Aaron's room at home very possibly resembled Chad's. But no, there was no way Aaron was *that* much of a slob—he always smelled good. He still owned clean clothes. (Even if his mom probably still did his laundry.)

"You have the weirdest look on your face."

Startled, I realized Julia was standing next to me, giggling. Natasha was there, too, and I felt a brief second of panic—had she seen me talking to Aaron? Not that I wasn't allowed to talk to him or anything. But I definitely didn't like the idea of Natasha seeing me blush when I handed him his folder.

"Hey! I didn't see you guys there," I said. Julia spun the dial on her locker.

"So what were you thinking about? You looked really grossed out."

"Oh, I was . . ." I hesitated, then realized I could tell

the truth, mostly. "I was thinking about my brother's room." I filled them in on Chad's disgusting laundry situation and my considerate and selfless offer.

"Wow, ten bucks a load," Julia said, laughing. "Not bad."

"He still hasn't accepted," I replied. "I'd rather just teach him to do it—money or no money, I don't want to do his laundry every week."

"Yeah, think about it," Natasha said. "You'd have to touch his *underwear*."

They both burst out laughing at my expression.

"Oh my God." I shook my head frantically. "No no no, I didn't even think about that. Okay, new plan. I'm telling him tonight that for every day he waits, I'm adding a dollar to the price of letting me teach him. Tomorrow, it's twenty-one bucks."

All morning, I tried not to dread band. I told myself that the Triangle of Extreme Awkward was all in my head—after all, Natasha and I were friends, Aaron had no idea I liked him, and everything with Owen was pretty much back to normal. Nothing to get anxious about. But apparently the butterflies knew something I didn't, because they were flapping away when I walked into the band hall.

Now that my excitement over being first chair had died down (at least a little), it felt really weird. I was even more hyperaware of every note Natasha played than usual, and I couldn't help but compare her playing to mine. I knew she was doing the same thing, even though she didn't say anything. And every time I flubbed something, even just the smallest mistake, I couldn't help but wonder if it was really, truly fair that I was first chair and she was second. Maybe I'd done better on my all-region audition than Natasha, but even though I hated to admit it, I still wasn't sure I was actually *better* than her.

I was putting my horn away, going over our last run-through of "Festive Yuletide" in my head and counting my mistakes, when Victoria's voice broke through my thoughts.

"Can I get directions to your place for tomorrow, Owen?"

"Yeah, just a sec." Owen grabbed a piece of paper and pencil, and Victoria noticed me watching.

"You're in this group, too, right, Holly?"

"What?"

"You know, to bake stuff for the game on Wednesday," Victoria said.

"Oh!" I ducked my head, pretending to search for something in my cubby. "Yeah, I'll be there."

I knew we were all meeting at Owen's tomorrow to get ready for the volleyball tournament. But for some reason, when Victoria asked Owen for directions I'd had this sudden mental image of the two of them playing *Prophets* and a very strong and unpleasant feeling had swept through me. Kind of like jealousy. Okay, maybe it *was* jealousy. Friendship jealousy, like the way I used to feel when Julia hung out with Natasha.

"So?" Owen said to me, once he'd handed the directions to Victoria. I glanced at him in surprise.

"So . . . what?"

He was giving me this expectant look, like I was supposed to know already. I just stared at him.

"*Cyborgs*. The ending," Owen said at last. "You said you were going to watch the first half over the break."

"Oh!" I stopped myself just in time from slapping my own forehead like a dork. "Right. I sort of, um . . . forgot." *And I'd rather watch it with you,* I wanted to add. But I figured that would probably freak him out.

Owen shrugged, turning back to his cubby. "Oh, okay." For some reason, he looked totally unsurprised. Like he knew I'd flake out.

"I started to!" I told him. "My brother had the DVD, and I put it in but then Julia called and—"

"Holly, don't worry about it." Owen's smile didn't quite reach his eyes. "It's not a big deal."

But it was, I could tell. Maybe it wasn't the movie, but there was something between me and Owen, something keeping our friendship from actually going back to normal. I watched him leave the cubbies, thinking hard. It couldn't just be my big overreaction to him asking me to the dance—he'd be over that by now. Was it that I'd said no? Did he want to go with me that bad?

I really didn't think that was it. Not unless Owen really did *like* me like me, which I was pretty sure he didn't. But whatever was bothering him, it definitely was a big deal.

𝄞

Even though we joked around like normal in science class, I was still nervous about asking Owen if our regular Thursday *Prophets* hang was back on. (And honestly, I was kind of worried about the concert programs, too. Without Owen's drawings, they'd be really lame.)

But I was too chicken to mention any of that to him, so we didn't talk about it. And that made going to his house after school on Tuesday to bake stuff for the fund-raiser kind of weird.

The Gradys had a big kitchen, but it was still pretty crowded with all of us there, even after Mrs. Grady gave everyone something to do. Brooke and I were making bowl after bowl of cookie dough, which we'd pass over to Dawn Palmer and Javier Vega, who rolled them into balls and placed them on baking sheets. Another small group on the other side of the kitchen was working on Mrs. Grady's cream-cheese brownies, and Owen was with everyone else at the table, frosting cupcakes. Trevor and Victoria went back and forth from the kitchen to the dining room, wrapping all the finished sweets and boxing them up. Mrs. Grady supervised all of us in between sliding trays in and out of the oven.

With the warm, sugary scent in the air and everyone chattering away, it was hard to feel bummed about anything. Still, I was very aware of Owen over at the table, and the fact that he hadn't said much more than "hello" to me. And when Mrs. Grady offered everyone drinks, I turned so red remembering how I'd spit my Coke out right here in the kitchen that she asked worriedly if I was getting sick, checking my forehead for signs of a fever.

"So are you excited about all-region?" Brooke asked, ripping open another bag of chocolate chips.

"Yes . . . although I'm starting to get nervous," I admitted. "I don't know how I ended up in the top band, seriously."

Brooke waved her hand dismissively. "Don't be nervous," she said. "I was in the second all-region band last year. It's fun, I promise."

I stopped stirring the batter, staring at her. "You made all-region last year?" As soon as the words were out of my mouth, I wanted to kick myself. Brooke had been third chair to me and Natasha all year, but I didn't mean to sound so obnoxious about it. "I mean—I'm not *surprised,* I just didn't know—"

Dumping the chips into the batter, Brooke laughed. "No worries, I'm not offended. I was alternate, and this guy from Forest Hill got sick, so I ended up getting to do it." She glanced at me. "I practiced for the auditions a lot more last year."

My face still warm, I focused on stirring again. "Sorry, I didn't mean it like that. Like I think you aren't good enough, or . . . I mean . . . you know . . ." I trailed off, groaning inwardly. *And the award for most awkward girl ever goes to . . .*

But Brooke was smiling. "It's okay! Yeah, I just spent so much time on elections this year that I kind of blew off the all-region music."

"Oh, that's right!" I vaguely remembered the student-council election last month. Brooke's name, the one right next to *President*, had been literally the only one I knew on the ballot. I'd voted for her, of course. "Well, it was worth it, I guess. How's it going?"

"Great! I love student council." Brooke swapped our full bowl with an empty one next to Dawn, then measured a few cups of flour. "It's crazy busy, though. A few weeks ago we all had to go to this leadership camp all weekend, which was so fun. And we've got a huge fund-raiser going on to help pay for all the big events this year, like both the dances, and the Earth Day activities, stuff like that. That's why I didn't offer to be in charge of this one," she added, shaking the bag of chocolate chips. "I've probably done enough fund-raising to buy myself a car, I swear."

I laughed, ignoring the knot in my stomach that had tightened at the mention of the dance. "So what was leadership camp like?"

For the next ten minutes, Brooke eagerly described everything they'd done that weekend—picnics, team-building games, some sort of practice marketing campaign where they'd designed logos and ads . . . Brooke and some of the others had even given speeches in front of almost a hundred other kids and counselors. By the time she finished, I was mentally trying to determine how hard it would be for me to run for student council next year and still keep up with band and all-region auditions. Student Council President Holly Mead. I could make business cards.

"Okay, let's put a hold on the cookies for a few minutes," Mrs. Grady called, taking another sheet from Dawn. "We've got a line of stuff waiting for the oven."

I went to the bathroom to wash my hands (the kitchen sink was overflowing with dirty bowls and cupcake tins) and passed the dining-room table, where Trevor was stacking brownies in Tupperware containers.

"Hey, Trevor."

"Hey," he replied. "I'm surprised you're here."

I stopped with my hand on the bathroom door, staring at him. He had a weird, smug little smile on his face. "What are you talking about?"

Trevor shrugged, fitting the lid on a container. "Nothing. Hey, you missed out big time the Thursday before Thanksgiving. We got to level ten."

It was like a slow punch that hit a few seconds later, hard. The Thursday before Thanksgiving—the day Owen had told me his stepsister had a recital and I couldn't come over to play *Prophets*. He *had* lied to me, after all.

I opened my mouth, closed it, and then went in the bathroom and shut the door firmly. But not before seeing how pleased Trevor looked at my reaction.

Leaning against the door, I stared at myself in the mirror. My face was all blotchy, some parts pale and some parts red.

I told myself that Trevor was a jerk—because he kind of was—and that maybe he was lying. Maybe Owen hadn't made up Megan's recital. Maybe this was all just a misunderstanding.

But telling myself that didn't make me feel any better, because I knew it wasn't true. I wasn't sure why, but it looked like Owen really didn't want to be friends anymore.

*T*he second volleyball game felt even more hectic than the first. Probably because this time, I was in the main gym instead of the auxiliary gym, and it looked twice as crowded. The line at our table was constant, and I was glad—all the work was a distraction from the fact that Aaron and Natasha were both right there with me, thanks to the booster parents who assigned everyone spots. Owen was back in the auxiliary gym, and so was Trevor. I was torn between hoping nothing traumatic happened to their table and kind of wishing Trevor would get knocked over with a volleyball again.

Julia was in the main gym, too—the woodwind table wasn't too far from ours. Next to her, Gabby kept hiding a tray under the table and replacing it with cookies, then putting it out again whenever a booster parent came around to check on them.

"Her mom's tofu bars," Natasha explained with a grin. "She made them last time, too. Gabby said people kept thinking they were cheesecake bars. Then they'd ask for their money back after they took a bite."

I laughed, handing a woman a brownie and her change and trying to ignore the way Aaron's arm kept brushing against Natasha's when he reached for the cash box. I was pretty sure it was intentional—he'd been standing on her other side ever since we set the table up, talking to her every chance he got. I was trying to ignore it. Weirdly, it seemed like Natasha was acting kind of standoffish with him, too. But that was probably just my imagination.

"If Mr. Gordon just took charge and baked all of their stuff, the woodwinds would win for sure," I said.

Natasha made a face. "They're winning, anyway. Sophie told me their average. And the percussionists aren't far behind them."

"Great." I sighed, opening another box of brownies. Thanks to Trevor, the brass section was so behind I wasn't sure we even had a chance at winning anymore.

I knew it wasn't actually Trevor's fault, but it made me feel better to blame him. Especially when I thought about how smug he looked at Owen's house yesterday. And besides, I'd really wanted to get to level ten first.

"So what do you recommend—the brownies or the cookies?"

Startled, I looked up to see a boy about my age at the front of the line. Correction: an extremely cute boy with thick black curls and very long eyelashes.

"Um . . ." Startled, I glanced down at the table. "The

brownies! Cream cheese and chocolate—they're *so* good."

"I'll take two," he said, handing me a few dollars. My face grew warm at the way he smiled at me, and I ducked my head to dig out a few coins from the box. *Pull it together*, I told myself.

"So are you from Forest Hill?" I asked, dropping the quarters in his hand.

"Yeah, my mom's the volleyball coach," he said. "This looks like a better fund-raiser than what our band's doing—we're selling scented candles. I've still got three boxes in my room. It smells like someone blew up a perfume store in there."

Natasha and I giggled. "So you're in band, too?" I asked. "What do you—?"

"*Excuse* me."

The three of us glanced over at two high-school girls standing behind the boy, arms crossed impatiently. The boy shrugged and smiled at me.

"See you later."

"Bye," I said, trying not to give the older girls dirty looks as they picked out their cupcakes. When they left, Natasha stuck her tongue out at their backs.

"He was really cute," she said in a low voice, nudging me with her elbow. On her other side, Aaron was deep in conversation with Gabe.

"Yeah, he was," I replied with a grin, hoping she hadn't noticed my eyes flicker in her boyfriend's direction. Or her almost-boyfriend. Her date. Whatever Aaron was.

But something else was occupying Natasha's attention. "Look!" she exclaimed, grabbing my shoulders and turning me around. My eyes widened when I saw Seth at the front of the line at the woodwind table, chatting with Julia.

"Wow, she wasn't lying—they actually *are* capable of having a real conversation," I said, and Natasha snickered. Even from here, I could tell Seth was blushing a little bit. Julia was nervous, too—she kept messing with the barrette holding the black curls away from her face. She was smiling, though.

"They're so cute!" Natasha said happily, and I had to agree. I opened my mouth to say so when I got a whiff of familiar cologne.

"Hey, we've got a lull in the line," said Aaron. My eyes went straight to his hand, which was touching the top of Natasha's arm. "I'm going to run over to the other gym and see what they've got left, okay?"

"Sure!" Natasha squeaked. I just nodded and turned my attention to rearranging the cupcakes that were left. Natasha started doing the same with the cookies. There was a weird silence between us, like we were right on the verge of talking. Neither of us said a word, though.

"Hey!"

Both Natasha and I jumped at the sound of Julia's voice.

"What's up?" I asked.

Julia waved a handful of bills. "We're low on fives—

can we swap a few tens with you guys?"

"Sure," said Natasha, holding her hand out. "I'll ask Gabe."

Once she was out of earshot, I poked Julia in the side. "We saw Seth holding up the line to talk to you," I said teasingly.

Julia smiled. "He's bought, like, eight cookies so far tonight," she admitted, and I laughed.

"So are you going to find him after the game?" I asked, scanning the bleachers until I found Seth. "I'm still holding you to our pact—and I don't know if you noticed, but Thanksgiving was kind of last week."

Glancing over her shoulder at him, Julia leaned closer to me. "Actually, he offered to stay after and help us clean up and stuff."

"Are you going to ask him to the dance?" I asked excitedly.

Natasha returned with a stack of fives, which she handed to Julia with a huge smile. "Who, Seth?"

"I don't know . . . okay, maybe I will." Julia gave us a mock stern look. "So you two *please* stay over here."

"What?" I cried. "Why?"

"Yeah, do you think we're going to embarrass you or something?" Natasha added.

Julia just grinned and shook her head. "Oh no, of course not."

After she left, Natasha and I went back to rearranging the table and chatting away without any of the awkwardness from earlier. I knew, though, that the second Aaron got back things would shift again. It seemed like that's how things were going to be with me and Natasha. Totally normal except for when Aaron was in the picture. The problem with that was if they really did start dating, he was going to be in the picture a lot more often.

$$\text{\clef{treble}}$$

"Nope."

Julia answered my unasked question the second I got to her locker Thursday morning. My mouth fell open.

"No, like he said no? Or no, you didn't ask him?"

"I didn't ask him." Julia sighed, twirling her combination. "He helped me carry a bunch of stuff out to Sophie's dad's car, but there were a ton of people around and then his parents and sister came out and he had to leave. But," she added, "I'm still going to do it, Holly. Today in PE, I swear."

So when the bell for fourth period rang, I hurried to the band hall. Natasha and I stood in front of Julia's cubby until the very last second, but she never showed up.

"Where is she?" Natasha whispered as we took our seats. Mr. Dante stepped onto the podium and started taking roll.

"I don't know," I whispered back. "Nothing happened first period?" Natasha and Julia had history together. Seth was in their class, too, and he and Julia had PE during second.

"No, nothing," Natasha replied. "They walked to gym together, though."

Then Mr. Dante started our warm-ups, and we couldn't speculate on Julia's absence anymore. But ten minutes into class, the door opened and she walked in.

I stared as Julia handed Mr. Dante a yellow slip of paper. "She's limping!" I said softly, and Natasha nodded. But when Julia sat down and noticed the two of us looking at her expectantly, she just grinned and shook her head. *I'll tell you later.*

After band, I helped Julia through the crowded halls while Natasha carried her stuff. The second the three of us sat down at our usual cafeteria table, Natasha put her hand on Julia's lunch bag to stop her from opening it. "No eating until you tell us what happened with Seth," she ordered, and Julia laughed.

"Okay." She glanced around the cafeteria. "But we've got to be quiet because he's right over there and I don't want him to think I'm making fun of him."

I looked over at Seth, three tables away. "Why would he think that?"

Julia pressed her lips together tightly, like she was trying not to laugh again. "So here's what happened. After Coach Hoffman told us to put everything up and go change, I went over to talk to Seth. He was telling me about something that happened in orchestra—I can't even remember what, I was just trying to figure out how to bring the dance up—and then, I don't know, I just kind of . . . blurted it out. I mean, I asked him."

Natasha bounced in her chair, and I beamed at Julia. "And?"

Julia ducked her head, her hand over her mouth. "Well," she said through barely suppressed giggles, "I probably should've mentioned that we were putting away the weights."

It took a few seconds for realization to dawn. My mouth dropped, and Natasha's eyes widened.

"Did he . . ."

"I guess I kind of caught him off guard," Julia said. "So, yeah. He dropped a ten-pound weight on my foot. *I said be quiet!*" she added frantically as Natasha and I cracked up.

"Wait, wait," I said, struggling to make my voice sound normal. "He said yes, right? About the dance?"

"Yup!"

"*After* he almost broke your foot?"

"Yes," Julia said, rolling her eyes.

Natasha gave me a sidelong glance. "But . . . will you be *able* to dance?" she asked, and we dissolved into laughter again.

"Stop, you guys!" But Julia was giggling, too. "It's fine—it's just a bruise. And he feels really bad."

I thought about all my awkward moments with Aaron. But I'd never done anything as embarrassing as nearly *breaking his foot.* Just imagining it gave me a rush of sympathy for Seth. Not enough to stop laughing about it, though.

"This is so great!" Natasha said, unwrapping her

sandwich and taking out a plastic knife and fork. "Can you believe the dance is next week?"

"I know!" Julia said excitedly. And then they both looked at me simultaneously, smiles gone, like the same thought had just occurred to them. Which it probably had, because I was thinking it, too. *The only one without a date.*

I shrugged, peeling my orange. "It's okay, guys. I'm going, and I'll have fun. Gabby doesn't have a date, either."

Julia looked relieved. "Yeah, it'll be great whether or not you have a date. Although, I mean, you could still ask someone. Or someone could still ask you!"

"I guess," I said, popping a piece of orange into my mouth. "I kind of wish I'd just said yes to Owen."

As soon as I said it, I shut my mouth. Too late, though. Natasha looked at me in surprise.

"Owen asked you to the dance?"

Julia and I shared a quick, panicked look. For the love—why had I said that out loud? I'd never told Natasha about Owen asking me, because that would involve explaining why I'd said no.

"Yeah," I said slowly. "Just as friends, I mean."

"Aww!" Natasha exclaimed. "That's so cute!"

Julia grinned. "That's what I said."

"So why—"

"But, anyway, I think I'd rather just go alone," I said quickly, picking at my orange. "Gabby made it sound fun." I shot Julia a pleading glance.

"Totally," she said immediately. "I bet a bunch of guys will be going without dates, too. Hey, do either of you have any shoes I could borrow? I thought my white flats would go with that dress I got, but it looks kind of blah."

"Yes, I have the perfect pair," Natasha replied, and she launched into a detailed description. I smiled gratefully at Julia. That was a close one. The last thing I wanted to do was tell Natasha—or anyone—about how sure I'd been that Aaron liked me.

Chapter Fourteen

*T*hat weekend, Mom took me to the mall and I found a dress at Milanie's—powder blue and shimmery, with this cool black lace over the skirt. But at the shoe store, I tried on, like, a hundred pairs and none of them looked right. I stood in front of the mirror in a light blue pair with short heels and black roses over the toes, holding the dress up in front of me.

"No."

I kicked them off, and Mom groaned, banging her head on the shelf she was leaning against.

"Holly, those were perfect."

"That's what you say about every pair," I said, putting the heels back in their box.

"Because they all look good," she retorted. "Are we going to have to go to another shoe store? I'm pretty sure you've tried on every pair here."

"Ha-ha." Hands on my hips, I scanned the shelves. Actually, I *had* tried on most of the dressier shoes. My eyes fell on something chunky and shiny in the corner.

"You're kidding, right?" Mom watched as I picked up the pair of silvery combat boots and plopped down on the stool. "We're only here to get shoes for the dance, not to—"

"That's what I'm doing!" I said, hopping up and walking—okay, stomping—to the mirror. The boots were heavy, in a nice way. They kind of made me feel like my *Prophets* character. Holding the dress in front of me, I grinned at my reflection. "Ready to kick some alien butt."

Mom looked like she feared for my sanity. "Huh?"

"Nothing," I said quickly, spinning around. "Can I get these?"

"For the dance?"

"Yes."

"Seriously?"

"Yes!"

It was kind of dumb, but thinking about the boots made me feel better about going to the dance alone. Like they were some sort of armor, or something. But even so, by Thursday I was starting to dread the whole thing all over again. Maybe because despite her attempt to hide it, Natasha was obviously excited about her first date with Aaron—she'd get so flustered and giggly every time he flirted with her. Or maybe it was because Julia was acting the same way about going out with Seth. I knew they were trying to play it down so they wouldn't hurt my feelings, which was nice, but it just made me feel defensive. Despite my "going to the dance alone is cool" attitude, I couldn't help feeling envious of them both.

And then there was Owen, who was just as nice as always all week, but still said nothing about hanging out after school. What I really wanted to do was just ask him if he still wanted to go with me. But now I was too afraid that would only make things weirder between us.

So I didn't say anything to him, either. About *Prophets* or the concert programs, which I'd started working on by myself. They looked . . . really, really not good.

Friday morning, I got to English, slouched down in my chair, and opened one of the fortune cookies I'd grabbed from the kitchen. Boots or no boots, I did not want to go to the dance.

"Bad morning for you, too, huh?" Gabby sat next to me and sighed. "The stupid vending machine gave me Skittles this morning." She popped a few into her mouth and made a face.

"If you don't like them, why are you eating them?"

"I like them, they're just not appropriate," Gabby replied. "Breakfast equals chocolate."

I laughed despite myself, unfolding the little slip of paper. DON'T AGONIZE—ORGANIZE! Overall, a pretty good life motto. I tucked it into my pocket.

"So what time are you getting to the dance tonight?"

"A bunch of us are meeting at my house at seven

thirty," she said. "My mom's taking us. Hey, want to come?"

The idea of walking into the gym with a group of girls was infinitely more appealing than walking in alone. Still . . .

"What?" Gabby said, squinting at me. "Hey, you're still going, right?"

I shrugged. "I guess. I don't know."

"Come on, Holly!" she cried. "I'm not letting you sit around all night moping about . . . him," she added in a lower voice, when I gave her a pointed look. "I know it's weird that he's going with Natasha, but—"

"But I need to get over it."

"Well, yeah."

"Yeah, I know." I sighed. "Okay, right, I'm going. Seven thirty?"

$$\oint$$

At 7:28, Mom pulled up to Gabby's house and gave me a kiss on the cheek.

"Have a great time!" she said. "I'll be parked outside the gym at ten thirty."

"Thanks, Mom!" I slid out of the car, shut the door, and clunked up the sidewalk. (Actually, I was already getting used to the weight of the combat boots. Although dancing in them was going to be interesting.)

"Hey, Holly!" Gabby beamed. "Come in, we've got— *nice!*" she cried, interrupting herself and staring at my boots. I grinned, wiggling one of my feet in the air.

"You like them?"

"They're awesome!" she exclaimed.

"Thanks!" I stepped closer to inspect her hair. "Wow, how'd you do this?"

Gabby's black hair was streaked with dark red, and all of its waviness was gone—it was half-pulled back and stick-straight.

"Victoria did it!" she said cheerfully, pulling me down the hall. "Everyone's back here."

Gabby's mom's bathroom was warm and crowded. Victoria waved to me in the mirror; she was busy taking curlers out of the blond hair of a girl I vaguely recognized from my math class last year. Next to them, two more girls were applying makeup. Leah was sitting on the closed toilet, painting her toenails with her foot propped up on the bathtub.

"Hi, Leah," I said, sitting gingerly on the edge of the tub. She glanced up in surprise.

"Holly!" she exclaimed. "I didn't know you were coming. Oh, wow, those are so cool!"

She pointed to my boots, and I smiled. "Thanks!"

We talked a little as Leah finished her toes and used a blow dryer to dry them. After a few minutes, Gabby's mom walked in with a huge bowl of popcorn, and Gabby pressed her hand to her heart like she was in shock.

"Popcorn?" she cried when her mom left, staring into the bowl. "Oh—it's that air-popped stuff. And no butter. Gross." But she ate half the bowl, anyway.

It was hard to dread the dance with everyone so excited and talkative. By the time we were all piling into Gabby's mom's van, I was really looking forward to it for the first time in weeks.

The gym actually looked pretty cool, considering it was . . . well, the gym. Shiny streamers were strung up along the walls, mini disco balls and giant sparkly snowflakes hung from the rafters, a DJ was already set up on the opposite side from the entrance, and several huge lights with color filters were fixed in all corners, making the whole place flash blue and white.

"Wow," I said, making a mental note to tell Brooke what a great job the student council had done.

"Yeah, not bad!" Gabby exclaimed. "Where's the food?"

We headed over to a long table covered with snack food and bowls of punch. While Gabby and the others talked and ate, I scanned the gym for Julia or Natasha, with no luck. It was already pretty crowded, though, and more people were coming through the entrance. I glanced over and was startled when Owen walked in. It didn't look like he had a date, either, which made me feel a weird combination of guilty and relieved.

The music got louder and the gym got darker very gradually, until after twenty minutes, trying to have a conversation was kind of pointless. The dance floor was pretty crowded, and Gabby was starting to look antsy.

"All right," she announced, stepping forward. "Let's see, who's the lucky guy . . ." Victoria, Leah, and I laughed as she made a show of looking around. "Mike!" she called, waving. "See you guys out there," Gabby said to us with a grin before walking over to where Mike Andrews stood with a few other guys. After a few seconds, she led him out onto the dance floor.

Leah sighed. "I wish I had her guts."

"Me too," I agreed. Victoria set down her cup of punch and took us both by the arm.

"Stop wishing and just come on," she said, pulling us into the dancing crowd.

The DJ played one fast song after another, and for the next hour I had so much fun, I couldn't remember why I hadn't wanted to come. We danced in a big group, forming a circle at one point and taking turns in the middle. Gabby and Victoria made everyone fall over laughing with a routine they'd obviously practiced. I danced with Mike for one song, then Rafael from my history class whose last name I didn't know, and then with Liam. At one point, I bumped into Julia, who looked like she was having a blast with Seth. (I couldn't resist teasing him a little bit about her foot. He blushed, but he was laughing, too.)

Natasha and Aaron were with a group on the other side of the dance floor; I recognized a few of the guys from the football team that Aaron usually ate lunch with, including Rick the Giant, who was, like, a full head taller than pretty much everyone around him. Natasha seemed to be having fun—but it was hard to tell from that distance, and I wasn't about to get any closer.

When the first slow song started, I told Liam I was getting a drink and left him to dance with Victoria. Hanging back next to the food table, I sipped punch and looked around to see who else was taking a break.

I spotted Owen with a few other kids near the bleachers. He saw me and sort of half-waved. I half-waved back, and he went back to talking. Chewing my lip, I wondered if maybe I should go ask him to dance. Would that be weird? Or would it help to break the tension between us?

Maybe it was Gabby's influence, but suddenly I felt like taking the chance. I set down my drink and started making my way through the crowd toward Owen. But by the time I got to the spot near the bleachers, he was nowhere to be seen. The kids he'd been talking to were still standing there, though. I recognized one from my PE class.

"Hey, Kyle, do you know where Owen went?" I asked, grateful that the slow song made it possible to hear.

Kyle shrugged and pointed. "That way, but he didn't say where he was going."

"Thanks."

I wandered around for a few minutes, looking for Owen. I couldn't shake the suspicion that he'd seen me coming and taken off just to avoid me.

Sighing, I peered at the bodies crowded on the dance floor, wondering if he was in there. That's when I saw Aaron and Natasha, dancing close. Really close.

Slowly, I turned away and headed back to the other side of the gym near the food table. A fast, thumping song started up, but I didn't feel like getting back on the dance floor just yet. I watched Gabby and the others for a few minutes, picking at a mini sandwich but not eating a bite.

"These are pretty good."

Next to me, Trevor was piling several of the little sandwiches on his plate. *Great. Just who I wanted to see.* I set my plate down and turned to go without saying anything.

"So where's your date?"

Stunned, I turned around and stared at Trevor. He smirked at me.

"I'm sorry, since when did you become such a jerk?" I snapped. "*Obviously* I didn't come with a date. Did you?"

Unperturbed, he stuffed a whole sandwich into his mouth. "No," he said, chewing. "But that's not my point."

"Oh, you have a point? I thought maybe you just liked making me feel bad."

Trevor rolled his eyes. "Everything really is all about you, isn't it?"

"Whatever." I turned to go, trying not to show how much he'd hurt my feelings. Trevor and I had always kind of picked on each other, but I never thought he disliked me this much.

"I told him so."

He mumbled it under his breath, but clearly I was supposed to hear it. Crossing my arms, I faced Trevor again.

"Told who what? You mean Owen?"

"Duh." Trevor poured more punch into his cup. "I told him you were lying."

"Lying?" I blinked in confusion. "I don't—what are you talking about?"

"He asked you to this, right?" Trevor waved his cup around, and I figured *this* meant the dance. "And you said no, because . . ."

I opened my mouth, but the words stuck in my throat. *I said I already had a date.*

Trevor nodded like I'd said it out loud. "And *do* you have a date? Nope. What a shocker."

Oh my God.

"I told him, asking you was stupid in the first place," Trevor went on. "And it was. And now you're here without a date, and it's obvious you lied and you don't even care that he knows it." He tossed his cup in the trash can next to the table. "And you think *I'm* the jerk," he added before walking away.

I felt sick. It wasn't like I'd forgotten the reason I'd said no to Owen, but when I found out that Aaron was going to the dance with Natasha, all I could think about was myself. From Owen's point of view, I'd told him I had a date, and never mentioned it again. And here I was, alone. He must have thought I'd just lied on the spot so I wouldn't have to go with him.

"Hey!"

I jumped when Julia appeared at my side, Seth not far behind her. They both looked flushed and happy. "Man, I need a drink," said Julia, grabbing a cup. Then she looked more closely at me. "Holly, are you feeling okay?"

"Yes . . . no," I said. "I need to talk to you about something for a minute. Come to the bathroom with me?"

"Sure," she said immediately. After telling Seth she'd be right back, Julia followed me out of the gym and into the restroom. I waited until the two girls at the sink had left before telling her the whole story.

"Yikes." Julia leaned against the wall, watching me pace back and forth in front of the stalls. "That's rough. Trevor didn't have to be so mean about it, though."

"I don't blame him," I said, and I meant it. "Owen's his best friend. I'd be pretty mad at any guy who lied and hurt your feelings like that."

"Holly, don't beat yourself up," Julia said firmly. "You thought you had a date, and it was easier to say so than explain the whole thing to Owen. And it wasn't like you were freaking out about the idea of going with him. I mean, if Owen had asked you *after* Aaron asked Natasha, you'd have said yes, right?"

"Yeah, but you're missing the point." I stopped in front of her, arms still crossed. "Owen has no idea I thought Aaron was going to ask me. He probably thinks I completely made it up."

"So just tell him what really happened!"

"I can't!" I yelled. "I mean . . . I *could*, but, oh my God, Julia, the whole thing about Aaron is so embarrassing. I don't want to tell *anyone*. Especially Owen."

Julia gave me a sympathetic look. "But I think it's the only way to fix things with him."

Groaning, I gently bumped my forehead against the wall a few times, and Julia laughed. I didn't want to admit it, but she was right. I had to tell Owen the truth. No matter how humiliating it was.

Chapter Fifteen

$\mathcal{I}$ had a week and a half until winter break. That meant ten days to figure out how to explain everything to Owen. Unless I wanted to put it off until school started again in January . . . but I couldn't stand the thought of obsessing over the whole thing during vacation.

So maybe it was because I was stressing out about seeing him in science, but during lunch on Monday, Natasha really started to irritate me.

"It was fun." That's all she'd say about the dance. No details, no hint of whether she'd be going on another date with Aaron. It was really unlike Natasha to be so tight-lipped, and while I knew she was just trying not to hurt my feelings, I was tired of the pity.

Julia, on the other hand, couldn't stop talking about Seth.

"And he called me Sunday! We talked for almost an hour. It's weird—he's a lot more talkative on the phone. Anyway, there's this Christmas-lights festival thing his family goes to every year, and he invited me to come with them! It's the day after the orchestra concert—oh, do you guys want to go to that with me? Seth's coming to the band concert, so I figure I should go to his, too . . ."

It was really cute, the way she kept rambling. And, okay, maybe a tiny bit annoying. But it looked like Julia officially had a boyfriend—I totally understood why she was so excited. So I just I smiled and nodded and ate my sandwich, wondering if this was how Natasha talked about Aaron when I wasn't around.

The next time Julia paused for breath, I turned to Natasha. "So are you and Aaron going to hang out over the break, too?"

I thought I sounded friendly, but Natasha flinched like I'd tried to hit her or something. Then she smiled quickly, although it looked forced. And she kept her eyes on her sandwich.

"Um, maybe!" she said, her voice kind of high. "We talked about doing something, but nothing definite yet. Besides, I'm going back to Georgetown for a week to see my grandparents. Are you guys going anywhere?"

Subject: changed. I couldn't help but roll my eyes, although neither of them noticed. Natasha was still focused on her sandwich, and Julia kept sneaking little glances over at Seth's table.

Well, at least I'd tried.

To make a blah day even more blah, science was horrible. Owen was the same—polite but distant—but now I was acutely aware of Trevor sitting a few lab stations away and shooting me dirty looks.

Okay, I didn't really see him giving me dirty looks. But he might as well have been. I stared at my lab packet, reading the same question over and over and not understanding a word.

"Hey, Owen?" I said finally. He glanced up.

"Yeah?"

I squeezed my pencil so hard I nearly broke it in half. "Um . . . what'd you get for number three?"

You have to tell him, I berated myself silently, pretending to scribble down the answer he gave me. But I couldn't do it here in the middle of science.

"Are you doing anything after school tomorrow?" Owen asked when I'd finished writing.

"No!" I said eagerly. "Why?"

"Well, the last volleyball game is Wednesday, and it's the third group's turn to bake," he told me. "But Gabe said we're so behind, we'd have to have a lot more stuff than we did at the first two games to have any chance of catching up. So my mom said she'd help us again, if you want to come. Victoria and Trevor will be there, and maybe a few others," he added quickly, like he was afraid I would think he meant just the two of us.

"Oh," I replied, a little deflated. "Yeah, that's a good idea. I'll be there."

We went back to work. Well, Owen went back to work, and I went back to pretending to work but really just doodling stuff all over a question about mitosis.

The tip of my pencil snapped off, and I set it down with a sigh.

When I shoved my hand into the front pocket of my backpack in search of another pencil, my fingers grazed a slip of paper. I pulled it out and unfolded it.

BE A GOOD FRIEND AND A FAIR ENEMY

Rolling my eyes, I shoved the fortune back in my bag. Stupid fortune. That was the one I'd opened in Chad's car on our way to the brass section fund-raiser meeting weeks ago. I froze, my hand still inside the pocket.

Maybe there was a way to fix things with Owen *and* help the brass section win the fund-raiser.

$

When Chad dropped me off at Owen's Tuesday afternoon on his way to work, I was even more nervous than usual.

"My shirt feels weird," he said, making a face and pulling at his collar. "Are you sure you showed me how to do this right?"

"Of course I did." I opened the door and reached into the backseat for the duffel bag I'd brought. "But I bet you forgot the dryer sheets."

"Did not," Chad said, but I could tell from his expression that I was right.

I rang the doorbell, gripping the duffel bag strap tightly. Mrs. Grady opened the door and smiled.

"Come in, Holly!" she said, stepping back. "Wow, I

feel like I never see you anymore. Been busy?"

"Um . . . yeah."

Mrs. Grady took the duffel bag from me and peeked inside. "Tell your mom I said thanks again for taking care of all this," she said. My mom had called Mrs. Grady this morning to fill her in on my plan. "It's a great idea, Holly. I really think it's going to do the trick."

"I hope so," I said anxiously. "Everyone's back here," Mrs. Grady said, and I followed her. When we entered the kitchen, my stomach dropped.

Owen had said "a few people," but apparently everyone wanted to make sure we didn't lose the competition. Victoria and Trevor were at the kitchen table with Dawn and Max; Liam, Brooke, and Gabe were leaning against the counter and talking . . . and Aaron and Natasha were getting mixing bowls and trays out of the cupboard. Natasha smiled nervously when she saw me.

"Hey!"

"Hi!" I said. "I didn't know you were coming." We hadn't even talked about it during lunch.

"Yeah, I didn't know about this until, um . . . after school." She looked back down at the cookie sheets in her hand. I knew what she meant—she'd been with Aaron after school, and he'd asked her to come. I wished she would just say so.

"Cool!" I smiled at her before walking over to the kitchen table, where I set the duffel bag down with a *thunk*. Owen glanced at it.

"What's that?"

I looked at Mrs. Grady in surprise. "You didn't tell them what we're doing?"

She grinned. "No way—this is your plan, you tell them!"

The others had gathered around the table by now, including Aaron and Natasha.

"What plan?" Aaron asked.

Everyone was looking at me. For a second, I wanted to squeak *Never mind!* and hide under the table. But then I saw Brooke smiling encouragingly, and I remembered my little student council president fantasy a few weeks ago. Unzipping the bag, I pulled out the recipe I'd printed out last night, along with a small plastic package.

"I think we should make fortune cookies," I told them. "My mom and I tried this recipe last night. They're really easy, and the thing is they only take, like, five minutes in the oven. We could make five hundred in an hour or two—maybe even more."

I unwrapped one of the cookies Mom and I made to show them. Mom had dipped half of it in melted chocolate, then coated the shell in yellow sprinkles. Brooke stuck her hand out.

"Can I open it?"

"Sure!"

I handed her the cookie, and she broke it open and took out the slip of paper inside. "'I'm trapped in a Chinese bakery, send help!'" she read with a grin, and everyone laughed.

"That's the other thing," I said, feeling more confident. "Some of you could write and print the fortunes, while the rest of us bake. So we can make them funny or stupid or whatever—you know, different from regular fortunes."

"I bet people would start talking about them at the game—you know, comparing fortunes and stuff," Brooke added. "We could sell of ton of these, like the percussionists did with that caramel popcorn. This is an awesome idea, Holly!"

"Definitely," Aaron agreed, and several others nodded.

"Thanks," I said, ducking my head to open the bag . . . and to hide my red face. "I've got all the ingredients here. Who wants to write the fortunes?"

While I unpacked cartons of eggs and bags of flour, sugar, and sprinkles to add to the supplies Mrs. Grady already had set out on the table, Victoria, Gabe, and Trevor raced upstairs to the game room to use Owen's computer. Mrs. Grady shook her head.

"Don't let any of Trevor's fortunes get in there without my approval first," she told me dryly. "I can only imagine what he'll try to get away with writing." I laughed, and so did Owen.

"This is a really good idea," he told me.

I shrugged. "You didn't think I was about to let us lose, did you?"

Owen smiled. "No way."

The next few hours flew by. We had a good

assembly line going, and soon we were mixing batter, dropping dollops on cookie sheets, and popping them in and out of the oven so fast I lost count of how many cookies we'd made. Victoria sprinted downstairs every few minutes with a handful of fortunes they'd printed and cut into slips. Natasha and I were reading them out loud before we placed them on the baked, flat discs, then folded them into cookies.

"'Got any mints? Your breath could use one.'"

"'Bad news—you're allergic to fortune cookies.'"

"'Someone you met last week is an alien in disguise.'"

"'When life hands you lemons, make lemon bars.' Or better yet, buy some from us!"

"'If you buy another cookie, it'll have a much better fortune.'"

"Here you go—the first one's mine." Victoria grinned, handing me the latest fortunes before hurrying back upstairs. I glanced at the one on top and laughed.

"'Watch out for rogue volleyballs.'"

Natasha giggled. "I bet Trevor loved that."

At eight o'clock, Mrs. Grady took out the last tray and turned off the oven. Once those were folded and dipped in sprinkles, it took another hour to wrap and box all of them. Aaron kept count while we worked, tracking the numbers in his notebook. When Max tossed the last wrapped cookie into a box, we all looked at Aaron expectantly.

"Hang on . . ." He typed a few numbers into a

calculator, and his eyes widened. "One thousand twenty-seven!"

"We made over a *thousand*?" Brooke exclaimed, and Aaron nodded. "Wow!"

"Hang on—we're selling these for fifty cents, right?" Victoria asked. "So this would be over five hundred dollars, not to mention all the stuff the other group is making at Javier's place!"

"If we sell them all," Aaron said. "Which I bet we do."

He grinned at me, and I tried not to look too pleased with myself. While everyone cleaned the counters and put the dishes away, talking excitedly, I opened the front pocket of my duffel bag and pulled out one of the fortune cookies I'd made last night. It was covered in blue sprinkles shaped like tiny stars. When I was sure no one was looking, I slipped out of the kitchen and up the stairs.

Owen's computer desk was a mess. I straightened up a little, throwing away the clips of paper on the floor and putting away the scissors Victoria and the others had left out. Then I carefully placed the fortune cookie on Owen's keyboard before heading back downstairs to join the others.

Chapter Sixteen

"**S**o what's this secret weapon Victoria keeps talking about?" Gabby demanded the second I got to English Wednesday morning.

"Secret weapon?"

"You know what I'm talking about—she said it was all your idea," Gabby said. "She said you guys think you might still win the fund-raiser competition somehow."

I smiled mysteriously. "I have no idea what she's talking about."

It was like the whole brass section had made a silent agreement not to tell anyone about the fortune cookies until the game that night. Julia bugged Natasha and me all through lunch, and neither of us said a word. Maybe after being so behind since the first game, we were all kind of enjoying having a secret weapon.

I was in a good mood when I walked into science, and not just because of the game. My stomach did a little flip as I set down my backpack.

"Hi, Owen!"

"Hey," he said with a smile. Then he went back to his sketchbook. I stared at him for a minute, waiting. He glanced up and blinked.

"What?"

"Didn't you . . . ?" I stopped, then shook my head. "Nothing."

He went back to doodling, and I opened my science book. *So long, good mood.* Was Owen really not going to say anything about the fortune cookie I'd left for him? There was no way he hadn't used his computer since yesterday evening. He must have seen it. And if he saw it, I was sure he would've opened it and read the fortune that was very obviously written by me.

But Owen didn't say a word about it all through science. So by the time I got to the gym that evening for the tournament, I wasn't nearly as confident as everyone else that my fortune-cookie plan would work. After all, the Owen plan had apparently been a total failure.

I ended up back in the auxiliary gym at a table with Brooke, Javier, and—*ugh*—Trevor. And it didn't take long for me to realize that the brass section just might win after all.

"This is *insane!*" Brooke cried, opening another box of cookies and handing eight to the two sixth-graders at the front of the line. "Holly, we've gone through at least a hundred of these already. We're so going to sell all of them."

"I hope so," I said, excited despite the whole Owen thing. He was in the main gym, along with Natasha and Victoria. Aaron was at the other brass section table in the auxiliary gym. After an hour, I saw him leave. When he came back a few minutes later, he headed straight for my table.

"They've already sold more than half of their fortune cookies in there!" he told us, and Brooke let out a little cheer. "This is awesome, Holly," Aaron added with a grin before heading back to his table.

And by the time the tournament was over, I had to agree. Not only did we sell all of the fortune cookies, but all of our brownies and cupcakes as well. Everyone from the brass section huddled around Gabe in the corner of the main gym as the crowd filed out. He'd been keeping track of the cash all night with the calculator on his phone, and now he was adding it all up.

"And the grand total is . . ." Gabe tapped his phone with a flourish and grinned. "Twelve hundred fifty-eight!"

"*Dollars?*" yelled Trevor in disbelief, and everyone laughed.

"That's more than we made at the first two games combined!" said Aaron.

"And it's because of those awesome fortune cookies," Brooke added, beaming at me. Then everyone was thanking me and patting me on the back, and while we cleaned up all the tables I couldn't stop smiling.

I was carrying a stack of boxes out to Mrs. Grady's

SUV when Owen caught up to me.

"Here," he said, taking a few of the boxes.

"Thanks!" My stomach started doing this weird leaping thing, like I was in an elevator that just dropped for a second.

"So something kind of funny happened when I got home from school today," Owen said. "Mom was upset with Megan because she got into the cookies."

"Oh no, really?"

"That's what Mom thought. She had a bunch of blue sprinkles stuck in her teeth."

I tripped a little on the curb. "Oh?"

"Megan kept saying she'd found it upstairs last night," Owen went on. "Mom and Steve thought she was lying—they were really mad. But she still had the fortune in her pocket, and when I saw it, I thought maybe she wasn't lying after all." Balancing the empty boxes carefully in one hand, Owen showed me the little slip of paper crumpled up in his other hand. I didn't have to read it to know what it said.

WILL YOU GO TO THE SPRING DANCE WITH ME? (PS— NINJAS WIN)

"Wow, interesting," I said, trying to sound surprised. "Even the fortune cookie knows the ending."

Owen laughed, shaking his head. "I thought you didn't watch it."

"I didn't," I admitted. "But the cyborgs look evil on the case, so I'm going with ninjas."

"Why didn't you just put it in and watch the first half?"

"Because I—I want to watch it with you." I kept my eyes on my shoes, feeling my cheeks warm up.

"Oh." Owen set the boxes in the trunk of his mom's car, then stepped back so I could put mine in. "Okay . . . how about sometime over winter break?"

"Really? *Ow!*" I straightened up too fast and banged the back of my head against the door. Wincing, I slammed the trunk closed and rubbed my head, trying to look nonchalant. "That sounds great."

"Cool." Owen smiled. "And I hope you're not too attached to that tank."

I made a face at him. "Trying to psyche me out won't work." But as we headed back across the parking lot, my stomach started doing that leaping thing. After a few seconds, I had to ask.

"So?"

He blinked. "So . . . what?"

I felt my cheeks turning red again as I pointed at the fortune still in his hand. "So, what's your answer?"

Owen looked at it, then at me. "Oh, wait—you're serious?"

He didn't say it meanly at all, but I winced, anyway. "Well, yeah."

"But the spring dance isn't until May. I thought you were kidding." Now his face was red, too.

"Neither is the science fair, and you're already making me work on that," I joked half-heartedly. Owen smiled a little, but didn't say anything. I took a deep breath.

"Here's the thing," I said, stopping outside of the school entrance. "I wish I'd said yes when you asked me to the dance. And I . . . I'm sorry I lied to you. That was wrong." Owen was staring at the ground, and so was I. But I made myself keep talking.

"It's not what you think, though. The thing is, I kind of thought I *did* have a date. I mean . . . there's this guy who I, um, like . . . and someone told me he said he was going to ask me to the dance. But it turned out he was talking about somebody else."

And right at that exact moment, the door swung open and bashed my arm.

"Oh, Holly! I'm so sorry!"

Natasha was backing out of the entrance, holding one end of a folding table. And of course—of *course*—Aaron was carrying the other end.

"It's okay!" I squeaked, grabbing the door with one hand and rubbing my sore elbow with the other. At least it was a distraction from my still-throbbing skull.

"Thanks, Holly," said Aaron as he passed.

"You're welcome." If anyone ever invented some sort of face lotion that prevented blushing, I'd so be all over it.

I kept holding the door open when Leah and Sophie came out carrying a few boxes, followed by two of the booster parents with another table. Neither Owen nor I spoke until I'd let the door swing shut and everyone was out of earshot. He was looking over at his mom's car, where Natasha and Aaron were loading the table in the back.

"They went to the dance together, right?"

"What?" I asked.

Owen pointed. "Aaron and Natasha. That's who you're talking about, isn't it."

Great. Closing my eyes, I wondered if my face had entered the purple zone yet. "Yeah."

"You like Aaron?"

"Yeah."

I waited several seconds before opening my eyes. But Owen was still watching the two of them over by the SUV.

"It doesn't look like Natasha likes him, though."

It was pretty much the last thing I'd expected him to say. Surprised, I looked across the parking lot as Aaron shut the back door of the car. Natasha stood a few feet away from him, her arms crossed, staring at the ground. Aaron said something to her, and she smiled and shook her head, then waved good-bye and hurried over to Leah and Sophie. Aaron stuck his hands in his pockets and slowly walked back toward the school. Even from here, it was easy to see he was pretty bummed.

"Oh, you're right," I said, forgetting my own embarrassment for a second. "But she *does* like him. That's weird."

"Are you sure she does?" Owen asked.

"Pretty sure, yeah." I turned to face him again. "Anyway, I'm really, *really* sorry about the whole dance thing. I shouldn't have lied to you."

"It's okay," Owen said. "And I'm sorry about what Trevor told you."

"Huh?"

Owen pulled the door open as Liam and Max came through carrying another table. "Trevor said he told you that we played *Prophets* that day I said you couldn't come over. You know, because of Megan's recital."

"He made that up?" I said hopefully.

"Well . . . no." Owen glanced down. "I mean, Megan really did have a recital, and I went to it. I wasn't lying about that. But the recital was right after school, so Trevor just came over a little later. I could've invited you, too, but I thought you . . . I don't know. I guess I just didn't. So I'm sorry, too."

I felt like about a hundred weights had been lifted off my shoulders. "It's okay."

Owen looked relieved, too. "Okay."

He pulled the door open and waited for me to walk through. I put my hands on my hips and glared at him.

"Hang on." I pointed at his hand again, the one still gripping the fortune. "You still haven't answered!"

Brushing the blond hair out of his eyes, Owen stared down at the fortune like he'd forgotten what it said.

"If you want to say no, it's okay," I said nervously, and he shook his head.

"No, it's just . . ." Owen gestured over to where Aaron was now helping Liam with the table. "It's not till May. Are you sure you don't want to wait and see if—"

"Know what Gabby told me?" I interrupted. "After I found out Aaron and Natasha were going together, she talked me into going to the dance by myself. She said it was better that way because if you got a date too far in advance, you might end up hating him—or her—after a while, but then you'd be stuck going with them, anyway. Which makes sense and all, but . . . well, I figure that can't happen with us. We'll still be friends in May, right?"

In the last ten seconds, Owen had probably blinked a blink for every single fortune cookie we'd sold. But he was smiling, too.

"Right," he said. "And yes. I mean, you know—yes, I'll go with you."

"Cool." I pulled the door open, feeling happier than I'd been in weeks. "Oh, wait! One more thing."

"Yeah."

"Please please please please *please*, will you still help me with the concert programs?" I asked. "Because I worked on them last weekend, and oh my God, Owen. They look. So. Lame."

Owen laughed. "Definitely."

Chapter Seventeen

*T*wo days before the winter concert, I got to the band hall early to put my horn up before first period. I noticed Mr. Dante in his office, and wondered if I could convince him to tell me who won the fund-raiser. (He insisted on keeping it a secret until the concert, when one of the booster parents would announce the winner right before we performed. All three sections were supposed to have Santa costumes ready—Mrs. Sutton, the drama teacher, was going to let us borrow stuff from the theater department.)

Everyone knew that the fortune cookies had been a huge success, but no one in the brass section had told anyone else in band exactly how much we'd made. It was going to be a close call, and I was dying to know if we'd managed to pull it off.

When I left the cubbies, I ran into Aaron. Literally.

"Oh, sorry!" I exclaimed, taking a few quick steps back (but not fast enough that I didn't get a whiff that sort of grapefruit-and-pine-tree scent that still made my stomach butterflies swing dance).

"My fault." Aaron leaned over to pick up the notebook he'd dropped. "Hey, I'm glad you're here—you got a second?"

"Sure."

"Hang on, where'd they go . . ." Aaron was rummaging around in his bag. I watched as a few pencils and a crumpled-up worksheet fell out, and fought the urge to grab his backpack, dump out its contents, and organize it properly. It would probably take most of first period.

"There!" he said triumphantly, and my eyes widened in surprise when he handed me three DVD cases—*Carrie* and the two *Watch the Fog* movies. "Sorry I've had them for so long."

"Oh, no problem." I stuck the cases in my bag and made a mental note to add them to the spreadsheet when I got home. "Did you get to watch any of them?"

"All of them," Aaron said. "They were great—I think the second *Watch the Fog* movie was my favorite. That scene where the doctor walks out of his office and doesn't see the dead kid crawling on the ceiling behind him . . . that was really freaky."

"That's my favorite part, too," I said eagerly. "And that's why the Asylum was so cool—that haunted house I told you about—because they *did* that. We got to this one room and this guy crawled right over our heads really fast, I don't know how he did it."

"All right, I'm definitely going next year." Aaron zipped up his bag. "You said you went with Natasha, right?"

"Yeah." As soon as he said her name, I got the weirdest feeling. Like I was doing something wrong, just by talking to him.

"You're pretty good friends with her?"

I wasn't sure I liked where this was going. "Um, yeah. Very."

"Right." Aaron slung his backpack on his shoulder. "Can I ask you something?"

Whoa, déjà vu. I had a sudden memory of standing right here with Aaron a few weeks ago when he'd said the same thing.

"Sure," I said, and in the next few seconds several things clicked into place.

"It's about Natasha," Aaron began.

(We'd been talking about *Carrie* and the winter dance. He'd said, "Speaking of, can I ask you something?" right before Liam had interrupted us, and I'd been so sure he was about to ask me out.)

"We went to the dance together . . ."

(But Natasha had been standing over by Julia's cubby. And I remembered Aaron glancing over in that direction. I just didn't realize at the time that he was looking at her.)

"And it was really cool—we had a great time. I mean, that's what I thought, and it seemed like she thought so, too."

(I'd told him Natasha came to the Asylum with me. He knew she was one of my best friends.)

"But ever since then, she's been acting kind of . . . different."

(He was thinking about asking Natasha to the dance, and he'd been about to ask me if she liked him.)

"Like she . . . I don't know. She's kind of avoiding me, and I don't know why. So I was wondering . . ."

(And now he was about to ask me again.)

"Do you know if Natasha likes me?"

I stood there, staring down at my shoes.

"Sorry, I know that's kind of a weird thing to ask," Aaron added. "It's just that I thought she did, but then sometimes it seems like she doesn't, and . . . well, you and I are friends, right? So I figured I'd ask you, because if she doesn't like me and I'm annoying her, I mean . . . I don't want to do that." He laughed a little, looking self-conscious.

A few weeks ago if Aaron had asked me all this, I would've wanted to crawl into a hole and cry for about a year. And while it certainly didn't feel great now, one thing he said stuck out more than all that stuff about Natasha: *You and I are friends, right?*

Even though I still felt hurt and embarrassed that I thought it was me he liked for so long, I was flattered. At the beginning of this semester, I couldn't even talk to Aaron without stammering or drooling. And now, somehow, we were friends.

And I was going to be a good friend, too. To him and to Natasha.

"She likes you," I said, looking directly at him. "She really does."

"Yeah?"

"Yeah." I nodded slowly, thinking. "And I know why she's been avoiding you. I mean, I think I do. I'll, um . . . I'll talk to her."

Aaron smiled, and I tried not to notice the parentheses. "Really?"

I nodded again. "Yeah, I will."

The theater department's storage room was pretty much the most amazingly wonderful place on earth. I stood in the doorway, mouth open. Mrs. Sutton glanced at me.

"Something wrong?"

"No," I breathed, gazing around at the colorful costumes neatly hung and arranged by theme; the stacks of clearly labeled bins filled with props; the long rack on the far wall, where at least two dozen wigs hung in color order, from bleached blond to blue-black. "This is, like . . . heaven."

Mrs. Sutton laughed. "Glad you like it. I'll be in my office if you need any help—just stop by before you leave so I know what you're borrowing."

"Okay. Thank you!" I added, right before the door swung closed behind her. After hesitating for just a second, I hurried over to the wigs, selected a bright red one with spiraling curls, and stood in front of the mirror, adjusting it and examining my reflection.

"It's *so* you."

I let out a little shriek and spun around to see Natasha in the doorway, laughing.

"Sorry," she said, joining me by the wigs. I twirled one of the curls around my finger, studying my reflection.

"You're right," I agreed. "I should go red."

Natasha grinned, grabbing a short black wig with a little red bow attached. "And *I* should go Snow White."

We spent about ten minutes trying on pretty much all of the wigs—and maybe a few costumes, too. Finally, I kicked off my red sequined heels and placed them back in their bin.

"We need to pick Mr. Dante's stuff," I said. Natasha glanced at me from where she stood in front of the mirror, modeling Peter Pan's outfit and holding a plastic samurai sword.

"Oh, fine."

"Actually, let me see that," I said, reaching for the sword. "I think we can use it."

"Do you know what you want him to wear?" Natasha asked.

"Sort of."

Right before school that morning, most of the brass section members met in the band hall and spent almost ten minutes arguing over exactly what kind of Santa we wanted Mr. Dante to dress up as if we won. Finally, he'd come out of his office to see what all the fuss was about.

"Why don't you vote?"

"We can't even decide on just two or three ideas to vote on," Aaron had told him. "Everybody wants something different."

"Well, you were in charge of this, right?" Mr. Dante had patted Aaron on the back with a grin. "Your call." He'd shut his office door behind him. Aaron had made a face.

"Hey," he had said suddenly, brightening. "If we win, it'll be because of those fortune cookies. And that was all Holly's idea. So I think she should get to pick the costume."

And miraculously, everyone had agreed. Although I think it was really just because we were all sick of arguing about it. So I'd invited Natasha to help me pick out something after school, and I'd had all afternoon to think about what I wanted to say to her.

As it turned out, I didn't have to worry about it.

"I need to talk to you about something, Holly."

"Oh. Okay," I said, setting down the Phantom of the Opera mask I'd been examining in one of the bins.

Natasha's face was already flushed. "I just wanted you to know that I, um . . . I don't like Aaron anymore. I mean, I like him, but . . . you know what I mean. Not *that* way. So we're not dating or anything like that."

I rummaged through another bin, this one filled with fake swords and knives. "Huh. Didn't you have fun with him at the dance?"

"Um . . ." Natasha picked at a loose thread on a black sash. "Yeah, I guess so."

"So you just . . . stopped liking him?"

"Yeah."

Laughing, I dropped a plastic machete into my bin and turned to face her.

"Natasha, you seriously don't have to do this."

"Do what?"

I smiled. "You like Aaron. And the only reason you're saying you don't is because you think you're hurting my feelings. But I promise—it's okay."

Natasha shook her head, her eyes still on the sash. "I know, you already said that. But that's not it. I really don't—"

"Really?" I waited until she looked up at me. "Come on, tell me the truth."

After several second, she sighed.

"Okay, the truth is . . ." Natasha chewed her lip. "The truth is I like him, and the dance was really, really great, and I—I really want to go out with him again. But," she said quickly when I opened my mouth, "what I want more than any of that is for things not to be weird between you and me. And me dating Aaron *would* make things weird, Holly."

"It won't," I said. "I promise."

"But—"

"Natasha!" I yelled. "I'm really *really really really* okay with it. *Really.*"

She looked at me nervously. "Really?"

After a few seconds, we both started laughing. I sat down cross-legged on the floor next to my bin, and Natasha joined me.

"I think it's too late, anyway," she said after we'd stopped giggling. "He asked me if I wanted to go to the movies this Saturday, and I said no. I'd be surprised if he ever asked me again."

"So you'll just have to ask him out," I said matter-of-factly. Natasha groaned.

"No way," she said. "That was the second time he's asked me on a date since the dance, and I said no both times. I can't just go up to him and be all 'Hey, I changed my mind!'"

"We'll figure something out." I pushed the sword bin aside and reached for another one. "Trust me, he'll say yes."

Natasha smiled at me. "Thanks, Holly."

"Anytime."

"So did Julia say anything to you about Seth's friends?"

"His friends?" I turned the sword over in my hands. "Probably. Is there anything Julia *hasn't* told us about Seth?"

Natasha giggled. "True. She does kind of talk about him a lot."

I gave her a Look. "*Kind of?*"

"Kind of . . . all the time . . ."

"Every second of every day . . ."

"Pretty much nonstop," Natasha finished, and we both laughed. "But I meant, has she told you about his orchestra friends? Apparently a few of them are pretty cute. I think that's the real reason she wants you to come to their concert."

"She wants to set me up?" I said in surprise.

Grinning, Natasha nodded. "Don't tell her I warned you, but she has this idea that you'll end up double-dating or something."

I rolled my eyes. "Oh, great."

"Hey, you never know, maybe one of them will be cool!" Natasha gave me an innocent look. "You might end up going to the spring dance with him. And Julia and Seth." She ducked when I threw a purple fedora at her.

"Well, too bad for her I already have a date for that." A second later, I had to fight the urge to slap myself on the forehead.

Natasha raised an eyebrow. "Hang on—do you?" She leaned forward, poking me in the arm with one of the fake knives. "Holly, do you seriously have a date for the spring dance already? That's not till the end of the year! Who is it?"

I really needed to stop blurting stuff out without thinking. "Fine," I said, knocking the knife away with the plastic sword. "But I swear, if you say aww, I'll . . ."

Natasha's eyes widened comically, and she pressed the sash against her mouth. "Owen?" she asked, but her voice was muffled behind the black fabric so it sounded like "oh-eh?"

"Yes. Just as friends," I added.

"*Wehdideeasoo?*"

"What?"

She lowered the sash, and I could tell she was trying not to laugh. "When did he ask you?"

"He didn't. I asked him. As *friends*."

Natasha pressed the sash back against her mouth, and I yanked it away.

"Stop looking at me like that!" I said, laughing. "Look, I was just trying to—" I stopped, still holding the sash.

"What's wrong?" Natasha asked, the corners of her mouth still twitching.

"Nothing," I said excitedly. "No, look—I've got an idea on how you can fix stuff with Aaron. Can you come over after we finish picking out the costume?"

"Sure. Why?"

I grinned. "We're going to make cookies."

Chapter Eighteen

*P*uffy sleeves. On the right top, they can be really cute. On dresses that your middle-school band probably bought twenty years ago, not so much.

Shaking my head, I stared at myself in the mirror in the girl's restroom. The dress was black and shiny, with a high waist and a skirt every bit as puffy as the sleeves. Sleeves which, by the way, were topped with black velvet bows.

"Maybe," I mused out loud, "we could see if Mr. Dante will let us do another fund-raiser for new uniforms."

Gabby and Julia nodded in agreement. "This is the same dress my cousin Elena wore when she was in band here. I mean, like, literally, I think it's the same exact one," Gabby said, making a face and pulling a loose thread off one of the bows.

"But yours almost looks cool with those boots, Holly," Julia pointed out.

I grinned, lifting my puffy skirt and sticking out a silvery combat boot. "True."

"I'm framing this program, by the way," Gabby said, waving hers at me in the mirror. I glanced down at my program, lying next to the sink. A giant UFO hovered over Millican Middle School, two Santa pilots visible through the front window. A green beam shone down from the bottom of the UFO into the school, pulling clarinets and trombones and drumsticks up out of the roof. Or maybe it was beaming them down into the school. Either way, it was pretty cool.

"Yeah, Owen did an awesome job," I agreed.

"Hey, where's Natasha?" asked Julia. "We're supposed to be warming up in five minutes."

"Don't know," I replied, running a brush through my hair. But I knew exactly where Natasha was.

She slipped past me a minute after the rest of us had taken our seats in the band hall. Mr. Dante was already on the podium, so I just gave her a look. *Did you do it?*

Natasha nodded, smiling nervously.

After our warm-ups, we headed into the auditorium toward the section the booster parents had reserved for all of the bands. As I followed Gabby down our row, I waved to my parents and Chad—who, amazingly, was wearing a clean shirt, although it looked like I needed to teach him how to use an iron.

We watched the beginners and the symphonic band, and in between songs Natasha and I whispered about the fortune cookie she'd hidden in Aaron's trumpet case. She was originally going to hide it in his cubby, but I told her if she did there'd be a good chance he wouldn't even find it until the end of the year. If then.

After the symphonic band had cleared the stage, Mrs. Park, the president of the band boosters, took the microphone.

"In just a minute, we'll conclude our program with the advanced band," she said. "But first, I'd like to take a few minutes to talk to you about our most recent fund-raiser."

"Mr. Dante's gone," Gabby whispered suddenly, and I scanned the stage.

"He must be putting on the costume I made," I whispered back, and Gabby made a face at me.

"Don't be so sure."

I stuck my tongue out at her, and she grinned. But really, I wasn't all that confident the brass section had won.

"As most of you know, our advanced band members have been hard at work raising money for their trip to New Orleans this spring," Mrs. Park was saying. "In the last several weeks, they've attended three of our volleyball team's tournaments, selling baked goods. That they made themselves," she added dryly. "I don't know about you, but I was shocked to learn my son even knew we had an oven."

Several parents laughed. In the row behind me, Liam groaned.

"This fund-raiser was particularly exciting, because it was also a competition," Mrs. Park went on. "Each section—woodwind, brass, and percussion—worked as a team, and the team with the highest average earned per member will get to design the band's shirts for their New Orleans trip. There's another prize, as well . . . but I'll get to that in a moment. Right now, I'd like the band to join me onstage."

As we filed onstage and took our seats, Mrs. Park told the audience more about our competition. Once the shuffling of chairs and the squeaks of music stands being adjusted had died down, she turned and smiled at us.

"Every section did a phenomenal job. The grand total from our fund-raiser was $6,845!"

"Whoa!" cried Gabby, over the cheers and applause. I grinned, but my fingers were drumming away nervously on the bell of my horn.

"And," Mrs. Park continued, "the average per student in each section was over one hundred thirty dollars! It was a close one, but one section managed to earn just a little bit more than the others. I think I'll let Mr. Dante come out before we announce the winner."

She gestured to the back of the auditorium, and through the darkness I could just make out another one of the booster parents opening the door. Laughter spread through the crowd, growing louder and louder. Half the band members onstage were standing out of their seats, trying to see. I squinted down the aisle as

Mr. Dante lumbered forward, then I grabbed Natasha's arm.

"That's our costume!" I yelled. "We won!"

Mr. Dante climbed the steps and headed toward the microphone to more laughter and catcalls. The Phantom of the Opera mask covered the right side of his face; I'd spray-painted it silver and glued a small fake ruby over the eye. He had the white hair and beard, but instead of a Santa hat, he'd tied a ninja headband around his head. And instead of a belt, he was wearing the black sash—it barely fit around the red Santa outfit I was pretty sure he'd stuffed with a pillow or two. One of the plastic samurai swords dangled at his side.

He bowed deeply, and everyone cheered. Shaking her head, Mrs. Park stepped forward again.

"Thanks to the extra effort they put into the last bake sale," she said, "the brass section was the winning team! But I honestly have no clue what they've done to poor Mr. Dante. Maybe someone could enlighten me?"

She looked at us expectantly, and most of us turned to look at Aaron, who was laughing.

"You picked it—you tell them," he said to me with a grin. So I stood up and clomped over to the microphone. The crowd fell silent, and I cleared my throat and smiled at Mr. Dante.

"He's a cyborg-ninja Santa Claus," I announced, and Mr. Dante slashed his samurai sword through the air and struck a karate pose. Giggling, I clomped back to my seat, high-fiving Owen when I passed him. Even

Trevor had joined in on the laughter.

Mr. Dante took his place in front of the band, and everyone sat up straight and lifted their instruments. Then he tapped the sword on the podium like a conductor's baton, and we cracked up again.

Playing turned out to be pretty hard with him dressed like that, waving the sword around. During "Festive Yuletide," he even cued the clarinets for their entrance with a karate kick, and I saw Julia duck her head to hide her laughter. But overall, I thought we sounded pretty good.

The booster parents had set up tables with bowls of punch and chips in the lobby for after the concert. "We were going to do cookies, but I think we're all kind of sick of those," I heard Mrs. Park say.

When I saw Natasha hovering in the entrance to the auditorium, I made a beeline for her.

"Well?" I asked eagerly.

She chewed her lip. "I don't know. I haven't seen him since we put our instruments up. I couldn't just stand in there and watch him open it, I was so nervous!"

We scanned the lobby, but no sign of Aaron.

"Maybe he didn't find it."

"He'll find it."

"Maybe he thinks I'm an idiot."

"No way," I said confidently.

"I don't know." Natasha was bouncing up and down on her toes, still peering through the crowd. "And I mean, Horror Hall? Seriously, Holly. Even if he says yes to that, I'll probably faint ten minutes into the movie and completely humiliate myself."

I rolled my eyes, grinning. "Come on, it won't be that scary, and I know for sure Aaron wants to go to this place. You can make him go to one of your sappy, predictable movies for a second date."

"Yeah, yeah." Natasha tried not to smile. "So where'd Julia go?"

"Where else?" I replied. "Over there, talking to Seth."

Natasha looked in the direction I was pointing, and she snickered. "So are you going to the orchestra concert with her tomorrow?"

"I think so."

She opened her mouth to respond, but before she could . . .

"Hey, Natasha?"

We both whirled around to face Aaron.

"Hi," Natasha squeaked.

I glanced around. "Um . . . I've got to go ask Julia something," I said in a too-cheerful voice. "See you guys!"

"Bye, Holly!" Natasha turned for a second, lowering her voice. "I'll call you later, okay?"

I nodded. Behind her, Aaron caught my eye. *Thanks*, he mouthed, holding up little slip of paper, and I smiled.

I actually had no idea exactly what Natasha had written on his fortune—I figured that was her business.

But her asking him on a date to Horror Hall was obviously my idea. No way would he say no to that.

I left them talking quietly in the corner. On the other side of the lobby, Julia and Seth were laughing about something. I hesitated, then headed over to where Owen's family stood a few feet from the snack bar. Steve was studying one of the programs.

"Hi, Holly!" Mrs. Grady said. "Congratulations— looks like those fortune cookies really did the trick!"

"Yup!" I agreed. "Thanks again for helping us make them."

Megan beamed up at me, her teeth coated with Oreos, and I giggled. Then I pointed to the program Steve was holding.

"Those came out pretty great, right?" I asked him. "Owen drew that."

Steve smiled. "I know he did. He's a talented kid. And this is"—he glanced at the crazy, UFO-driving Santas again—"very, very weird. Good weird," he added quickly, and Mrs. Grady laughed.

"I can't wait to see what he comes up with for the band T-shirts," she said.

"Me too," I agreed. "They're going to rock." Glancing up, I saw Owen and Trevor piling chips into their napkins at the snack bar. "I'll be right back—I'm going to get a drink."

I waved to Megan, who waved back, her cheeks bulging with more Oreos. Grabbing a cup, I headed to the punch bowl.

"Hey, Holly," said Trevor.

"Hi," I replied, trying not to sound too taken aback that he was talking to me.

"That was pretty cool," Trevor said, filling his napkin with chips. He glanced at me. "Dante's costume, I mean."

I smiled at him. "Glad you liked it."

Trevor shrugged.

"He's still wearing it." Owen pointed, and I saw Mr. Dante over by the main office, taking pictures with some of the beginner-band members. He was still striking different karate poses and waving the samurai sword around. As we watched, he started a duel with a drumstick-wielding percussionist.

"Any T-shirt ideas yet?" I asked Owen, who was piling handfuls of crackers into a napkin.

"Some," he said, nodding. "I'll show you."

"Steve liked the programs," I informed him.

"Yeah, I know," Owen said. "I showed him one after we got them printed. He said they were good." He paused, making a face. "Then he asked me when baseball tryouts were."

I groaned, and Trevor snorted.

"Dude, you're not *actually* trying out for that, are you?"

While they talked, I glanced around the foyer again. Natasha and Aaron were in the same spot I'd left them, talking and laughing. Not too far from them, Julia and Seth were holding hands. I smiled to myself as I reached for a handful of chips. Even from here, I could tell that Seth was blushing a little bit.

"Anyway, are you guys still coming over Thursday?" Owen asked. "I bet we can hit level fifteen."

"Sure," said Trevor immediately. I grinned at Owen before popping a chip into my mouth.

"I wouldn't miss it."

Acknowledgments

As always, enormous thanks to my editor and fellow band geek, Jordan Hamessley, for being one of those rare folks I can talk shop with about both writing *and* music. And a huge thank you to editor in chief Sarah Fabiny for her constant support.

Thank you to superagent Sarah Davies for being the best advocate an author could ever ask for, and for being consistently reliable and supportive in an industry with wild ups and downs.

Thank you to art director extraordinaire Giuseppe Castellano and designer extraordinaire Mallory Grigg for continuing to blow my mind with the amount of work and love they put into this series. And thank you to Genevieve Kote for the incredible illustrations that bring Holly and her band-geeky world to life.

Thank you to Amanda Hannah, Kate Hart, Kirsten Hubbard, and Kaitlin Ward, for . . . reasons. Many, many infinite reasons.

Thank you to my parents, John and Mary, and my sister, Heather, for the never-ending support and enthusiasm. Oh, and the gumbo—thanks for the gumbo.

Thank you to Josh, for pulling me back into the music world when I start to drift, and for all the days spent dream-planning at the diner. And thank you to Adi, for making sure I tear myself away from the laptop at least a few times a day.

And thank you to all the friends I've made because of band, whether it was school, rock, jazz, reggae, calypso, or anything else. Hope we get to play together again.

Coming Soon!

I ♥ Band!

#3 Sleepovers, Solos, and Sheet Music

Turn the page for a sneak peek!

Chapter One

*T*he second half of seventh grade should come with some sort of warning: *Congratulations! You're exactly halfway through middle school, so everything's about to get twice as hard.*

Apparently all my teachers came back from winter break last month thinking we were high-schoolers or something. My English teacher, Mr. Franks, announced that we'd be writing two essays a week—two!—*plus* a big research paper due later this semester. In science, Mrs. Driscoll had given us a crazy schedule for our science fair projects, and our labs were getting ridiculous—as if any day now she'd be asking us to find a cure for the common cold. And the way Mr. Hernandez kept drilling us on verb conjugations, I was pretty sure he was expecting us to be fluent in Spanish by the end of the year.

But that was nothing compared to band.

My music folder was *stuffed*: a thick packet full of

new scales and exercises. "Labyrinthine Dances"—this ridiculously hard piece that we'd been rehearsing since the beginning of the year for a contest that wasn't even until April. Three more songs we'd be performing on our band trip to New Orleans a month from now. My music for the all-region concert this weekend, which sent a flurry of excited-but-nervous butterflies flitting around my stomach every time I looked at it. And "Pastorale for Horn," my solo for Solo and Ensemble Competition, which I'd perform in front of a judge for a rating and (hopefully) a medal.

As if all that wasn't enough, now Mr. Dante was handing out even *more*.

"'Triptych,'" he said, reaching across the saxes to hand me a sheet of music. "Brass trio—this one will be Holly, Aaron, and Liam. Next up, let's see . . . 'Canon in A,' woodwind quartet: Julia, Sophie, David, and Luis."

While Mr. Dante continued handing out parts, I stared at my music. The butterflies started swing dancing.

"Triptych" made all those other songs look like "Three Blind Mice."

"Wicked," Gabby said next to me, and I glanced at her music. It looked just as hard as mine, but Gabby could totally handle it. She was amazing.

I mean, I was good, too. I was actually first chair French horn in the advanced band. But still . . .

"When exactly is Solo and Ensemble again?" I asked her, even though I knew the answer.

"Last weekend of February," Gabby replied. "Right before the band trip."

"Less than a month," I said, drumming my fingers on the bell of my horn. "We have less than a *month*."

On my other side, Natasha Prynne was staring at her own music, her eyes wide. "This is crazy."

"I know," I agreed. Honestly, I was kind of relieved that she was worried, too. Up until all-region auditions last November, Natasha had been first chair in our section. Then I'd made the top all-region band, while Natasha was in the second band. And even though I practiced a lot, part of me still thought it was some sort of fluke. I was a really good horn player, but Natasha was pretty fantastic, too.

Someone tapped me on the shoulder, and the smell of cologne made my stomach flip for an entirely different reason.

"Hey, Holly, do you think we could practice this before school?" Aaron Cook asked, and I saw he was holding the trumpet part to "Triptych." "I had baseball tryouts yesterday, and it looks like practice is going to be pretty much every day after school for the next month or so."

"Sure!" I said, trying not to sound too enthusiastic. "How about Wednesdays and Fridays?"

"Works for me," Aaron replied. "I'll check with Liam." He smiled at Natasha. "So who's in your ensemble?"

Natasha half-turned in her chair to face him. "Um,

Gabe, Victoria, and . . . I think Max." Her voice was a little higher than normal.

"Cool!"

Before Aaron could say anything else, Mr. Dante stepped back up onto the podium. I glanced at Natasha; her cheeks were pink. I hoped mine weren't.

Last semester, I'd had a pretty big crush on Aaron, and Natasha knew it. And now she was kind of dating him. Which was totally fine with me—I'd actually helped set them up, because I knew they liked one another. But being in an ensemble with my friend's almost-boyfriend who I used to like (and was sort of still getting over) . . . yeah, that could be a little bit way awkward.

Maybe that was another part of making it halfway through middle school. *Congratulations! All your friendships are about to get twice as complicated.*

$$\oint$$

Lunch was now total proof of that. It used to be pretty simple—me, Julia, and Natasha at our regular table. But now, lunch involved boys.

Specifically, Seth Anderson. He was Julia's boyfriend. Not almost-boyfriend, like Natasha and Aaron. *Boyfriend* boyfriend. So he ate lunch with us. Which was totally cool, don't get me wrong—I liked Seth a lot. He played cello in the school orchestra, he was really into photography, and when he found out about my obsession with horror movies, he let me borrow his book of Edgar Allan Poe stories (which was *amazing* and had some pretty wicked illustrations, too).

Still, lunch was different once he started eating with us. Because Julia was different.

"That test in Spanish yesterday was really hard," Natasha said as we left the cubby room. I nodded in agreement.

"Mr. Hernandez is losing it, I swear." I held the band-hall door open for her and Julia, and we headed to the cafeteria together. "I didn't recognize half of those vocabulary words."

"That's what Seth said," Julia chimed in. "He has Mr. Hernandez seventh period."

"Hey, I forgot to tell you!" Natasha said suddenly, nudging me. "We ordered Lotus Garden last night for dinner, and Chad delivered it! My dad gave him a five-dollar tip, and I said that would cover half a load of laundry. He looked pretty mad."

Julia and I laughed. Not only was my brother pretty much the messiest human being on the planet, he refused to learn how to operate a washing machine. At ten bucks a load, I was making decent money keeping his clothes clean—although sometimes I wondered if it was worth it. I mean, doing his laundry meant dealing with underwear. Which was why I wore rubber gloves.

"I might up my price," I told them. "Last weekend he played football for, like, six straight hours. Oh my God, that load of clothes—I almost passed out from the smell, I swear."

"Still, the extra money must be nice," Julia said. "Seth's been doing yard work for his neighbors, but I bet you make more doing your brother's laundry. Oh, did I tell you guys I met Seth's sister over the break? She's a music major! She plays piano, but she's a singer, too, and . . ."

Julia kept talking, and Natasha and I shared an amused look. Amused, and maybe a little exasperated, too. Lately it seemed like it was pretty much impossible to talk about anything without Julia bringing up Seth.

That was probably why we only spent half our lunch period together lately. I mean, it wasn't *just* because of Julia. Aaron had lunch then, too, and Natasha usually went and sat with him after she finished eating. She'd been worried about leaving me at first—and honestly, it might have bothered me if I'd been stuck as a third wheel with Julia and Seth. But I had someone else I could sit with, too.

"See you in seventh?" I asked Julia, standing and crumpling my lunch bag. Natasha was on her feet, too, brushing the crumbs off her skirt.

Julia nodded. "Tell Owen I said hi."

I glanced at her, because she sounded like she was trying not to laugh. "What?"

"What?" Julia asked innocently. "Nothing!"

"She thinks you like Owen," Seth told me. Julia smacked his arm, and Natasha giggled.

I rolled my eyes. Right before winter break, I'd asked my friend Owen Reynolds to the spring dance.

For whatever reason, Julia and Natasha both found that funny. No matter how many times I told them it wasn't a *date* date.

"I do like Owen." I smiled at Seth. "That's why we're friends."

Julia gave me an innocent look. "For now."

Natasha walked to the trash cans with me, still grinning. "She's just giving you a hard time."

"I know." I tossed my bag into the garbage. "Kind of weird that she talked about me and Owen with Seth, though."

"Well," Natasha pointed out, "she can't talk to Seth about *Seth*."

I snickered. "True." And honestly, I was kind of flattered. Julia had spent so much time lately talking about her boyfriend, I'd been wondering if she was even interested in the rest of us anymore.

Natasha headed off to Aaron's table. Most of his friends were in eighth grade, like him. I didn't really know any of them, but Natasha said they were pretty nice. She didn't talk about them much. Actually, she didn't even talk about Aaron much, and not just in comparison to Julia.

I plunked down next to Owen, who was shuffling a stack of Warlock game cards. "I'm in!"

"Good timing," Owen said, smiling. He handed me half of his stack. Across the table, Trevor Wells sighed.

"You know the reason you keep losing is because you split your cards with her," he informed Owen. "Last week she got your draught of death card."

Owen shrugged, brushing the blond hair out of his eyes. "So?"

"So, you would've won if you'd had it."

"Come on, Trevor." I flipped through my stack and glanced at the goblin-chief card he'd tossed in the center of the table. "It's not about winning and losing, it's about having fun. And freezing your goblin chief with my ice sword is really, really fun."

I placed my card on top of Trevor's with a flourish, and everyone laughed. Everyone except Trevor, of course. He was always a really sore loser.

"Everyone" was Owen, Max Foster (who played trombone in advanced band, like Trevor), and Brent McEwan and Erin Peale from fifth-period science. And today there was a new guy who I vaguely recognized from my history class last year. Keith or Kyle or something like that.

Ten minutes later, Max was pretty much destroying all of us, which was nothing new. (Although Owen and I really would have had a better chance if we'd each had a full deck of cards.) And I'd managed to snag one of Trevor's undead-warrior cards, along with the goblin chief. When Max scored his shield cloak, Trevor threw his cards down in frustration and started arguing with him.

"Guess that's the end of that game." I handed Owen back his cards.

"The bell's about to ring, anyway," he said,

wrapping a rubber band around the deck and tucking them into his backpack. Out of habit, I glanced over at Aaron's table. They were all laughing at something—all except for Natasha. She was smiling, though. I squinted, trying to read her expression. It might have been my imagination, but sometimes I thought Natasha looked a little uncomfortable sitting with Aaron's friends.

"You okay?" Owen asked.

"What?" I glanced at him, startled, and realized he'd seen me staring. And since Owen knew I liked—used to like—Aaron, that's probably who he thought I was staring at. "No! I mean, yeah. I'm okay." My face felt a little warm, so I ducked down to pick up my backpack. "Do you have our proposal for Mrs. Driscoll?"

"Yup."

"What are you guys doing for the science fair?" Erin asked, and Owen immediately launched into a detailed description of our project. I was pretty excited about it, too, actually—I mean, it was about aliens on Mars, how could that not be cool? Right now I was too distracted to think about it, though. The science fair wasn't until May, but that weekend I had all-region band, where I'd be performing with a bunch of kids from other middle schools. And we'd only have two rehearsals to learn the music. Then there was the contest on the band trip to worry about, plus my solo for Solo and Ensemble. Oh, and now I was supposed to learn this crazy hard music for a trio with my former crush who was now kinda dating one of my best friends.

My other classes might have gotten more intense, but band was officially *insane*.

About the Author

Michelle Schusterman is a former band director and forever band geek, starting back in the sixth grade when she first picked up a pair of drumsticks. Now she writes books, screenplays, and music in New York City, where she lives with her husband (and bandmate) and their chocolate Lab (who is more of a vocalist).